Annemarie Nikolaus: Back onto the Dance Floor
Quick, quick, slow – Lietzensee Dance Club

Back onto th Dance Floor. *Quick, quick, slow – Lietzensee Dance Club*
Copyright © 2015-2019 Annemarie Nikolaus
Originally published in German as: Zurück aufs Parkett. *Quick, quick, slow –*
Tanzclub Litzensee
F-03240 Tronget/Allier
Cover: Design Tine Sprandel 2015-2019, Foto https://pixabay.com/de/mittelalter-
tanz-geschichte-276019/ PublicDomainPictures 2013, Pixabay License

ISBN (Paperback) 9782902412303
Annemarie Nikolaus, Tronget/France

Annemarie Nikolaus

Back onto the Dance Floor

Quick, quick, slow – Lietzensee Dance Club

Novel

1

Dumbfounded, Friederike Lagrange was gazing after her grand-daughter: Madeline had squeezed her Balinese mask under her arm and thus apparently declared the Carnival ball was over.

George Lagrange grabbed Friederike's hand. "Don't wor-ry, she'll be right back." He bent over to her ear to defy the music that was starting again. The combo had replaced the piano player and now it got loud. A ball in the Lietzensee Dance Club was not meant for conversation. "In her all-time sandals she won't get far in the snow."

"There you know Madeline rather badly, George." Be-sides, Madeline was wearing boots to her pirate costume.

Robert Merck, former dance partner of Madeline, joined them at their table; he sat on the place where Madeline had just been. "Really a pity. Your granddaughter is wasting her talent with this outlandish Ring o' Roses."

Irritated, Friederike raised her eyebrows. "The square dance group keeps bringing good money to the club."

"Robert, I think you're wasting your time with us. Didn't you come here to dance?"

"I was counting on Madeline." He grinned at George. "I don't want to change club. But I haven't found a permanent partner yet."

"Then you should dance now all the more," George said. "It's the best way to find a new partner."

Robert's gaze went through the hall. "I don't want to mess with anyone by assuming the role of competitor." His gaze remained fixed on Friederike. He sighed. "Tomorrow I would hardly recognize anyone of them anyway."

What kind of argument was that? Instinctively she shook her head.

George also shook his head. "You shouldn't worry about that. One who is satisfied with her partner will certainly not leave him." He squeezed Friederike's hand. "It's a bit like being married."

" Well, yes, in that case..." Robert's smile suddenly became somewhat roguish. "Then you're certainly not angry with me, George." He stood and bowed to Friederike in perfect form. "May I ask you to the war dance, beautiful squaw?"

She laughed. Robert was amusing; it was a pity that Madeline didn't get along with him.

"My wife doesn't dance!" George sounded unfriendly, hard.

Robert gasped in surprise. "Is that true?"

"I'd really like to dance. But that..." Friederike pointed to the dance floor where the couples were working their way through a hot samba. "That's too tiring for me."

For a moment Robert seemed dismayed, but then he stretched out his hand with a smile. "Then we wait for one of the slow waltzes. Don't you also have a dance card? I'll sign in if George has left anything free."

Now it was up to George to look dismayed. He cleared his throat, but before he could say anything, Friederike pushed her dance card over the table to Robert.

He reached for the pencil Madeline had left and opened the card. "But it's still all empty!" He grinned at George. "You thought you didn't have a competitor?"

"Friederike doesn't dance at all anymore."

She began to get angry about George. "This is a good evening to start again. Robert is certainly a considerate dancer." Madeline, however, had said something completely different about him. Therefore she didn't dance with him anymore. But he could surely do differently when it wouldn't matter. And from her he wanted nothing, if he didn't happen to need a new grandmother.

George apparently was going to puff himself up. So she kicked him under the table against the shin, to keep his mouth shut. "I would be happy to have two such wonderful dance partners tonight." She pointed to two slow waltzes and a slowfox in her dance card. "Sign in here, Robert."

He looked at George, but he managed to look unmoved. So Robert signed in. Then he gave the card to George and held the pencil out to him.

More than hesitantly George took both and then studied the card, mumbling the individual dances with a question mark in his voice. At the first rumba he looked up. "The rumba was always your favorite dance. But that will certainly be too exhausting for you."

"Too exhausting? A simple rumba?" Robert looked incredulous from George to her. "It's Carnival, not April Fools' Day."

"I had a serious car accident, Robert. It took many years until I could actually walk again."

George's mien was closing more and more. "And when Friederike overexerts herself, she still limps."

"I'm very sorry about that." Robert's voice held sincere consternation; this young man really wasn't that bad. "I'll be certainly careful, that I don't overexert you." He put two fingers on her hand. "But do you really want to dance with me?"

Didn't she say that clearly enough? "If I don't try, I won't find out if I can do it again." She looked at George. "It would be wonderful if we could dance again like we used to." Maybe then they would get back even more from the old days; not just dancing.

"Well. A few steps..." George put the pencil on the rumba. "But it may rob you of the last dance, Robert. I doubt Friederike will hold out that long." He frowned. "You'll say it immediately when your leg starts to hurt, don't you?"

She nodded. But she wouldn't do that for sure. She wasn't one to throw in the towel at the first ailment. Otherwise she would still be in a wheelchair. That he didn't realize that – men!

Once the first bars of the slow waltz sounded, Robert stood and pushed the saber in his sash aside. "Are you ready, Friederike?"

And how she was ready! The moccasins were flat and snuggled softly to her feet. She moved in them as if walking on clouds.

Robert led her with gentle pressure into the basic step; his mouth was close to her ear. "We don't want to embarrass ourselves, right? Tell me what you dare to dance."

She half closed her eyes, let herself be guided for two bars by the music and by Robert. "I think, with you I can manage all the steps."

He laughed quietly. "I didn't assume you had forgotten anything. But if I tire you with the first dance, I have to do without the other two."

"I'll tell you if it gets too much for me." This explanation earned her a more than sceptical look. So he had noticed that she had lied to George earlier. She smiled at him. "Really!"

They arrived at the first corner of the hall and he led her into a spin, watching the expression on her face. What he saw may have reassured him, for his grip became lighter. He relaxed and immediately spun her again.

Friederike closed her eyes for a moment. "Until just now, I didn't know how much I really missed this."

"And you were right to try. You're as supple as a young girl." He grinned broadly. "But much more obedient."

Was he talking about Madeline? Madeline had almost scratched out his eyes at the beginning of the evening. She laughed spontaneously. "Sometimes it's worth being obedient." For once she did not understand her granddaughter. With her bitchiness she had achieved nothing but to spoil this evening for herself.

Robert became more courageous and danced a long passage, which demanded a faster step sequence of her. "Bravo," he whispered into her ear, but then suddenly stiffened, his eyes widening.

Breaking the rules, she turned her head to the side to see where he was looking. She met George's gaze, who apparently followed them with narrowed eyes. In the next spin she raised her hand halfway from Robert's upper arm to wave to him.

When the dance was over, she sighed contentedly.

"Relieved"? Robert put her hand in the crook of his arm to bring her back to the table.

"Yes, but unlike you might think: I'm glad I dared."

"You seem to know very well what you can ask of yourself. I don't even know why George is so worried!"

But now she had to defend him. "He has been through a lot during my rehabilitation. There were a few setbacks. In the beginning. At that time I actually didn't know what I could expect of me and what I couldn't do."

"And that's why he's wrapping you in cotton wool now."

Their arrival at the table absolved her of an answer.

George reached out to her and prevented her from sitting immediately. "Everything all right?" He touched her neck. "You're bathed in sweat."

"I was even before the dance. My costume is too heavy for here. They have heated the hall for the half-naked."

George immediately jumped on the diversion. "You should still remember that the Latin dancers are always half-naked. Don't you?

"Sure. And we were always grateful for appropriately

warm rooms." She shrugged. "I don't complain. I just told you why I sweat."

He finally let go of her and she sat, more than happy that she could now relieve her leg. She reached for her wine glass and at that deliberately pushed the dance card off the table. When she picked it up, she wanted to look inconspicuously how long she could rest. But Robert was attentive and faster than her. He put the card in front of her even before she had put down her glass. But he opened the card and took a look. Had he possibly seen through her again or did he just want to know for himself when the next dance would come for them?

Cautiously, she moved her leg under the table. If she could massage the thigh a little, the pulling pain would certainly stop. But she didn't dare go with her hand under the table; George would notice and know what it meant. And make her a scene.

Three dances later came the next slow waltz. After two spins, the pain in her leg became more pronounced. True to her promise, she tilted her head closer to Robert and whispered: "We better do this a little less swinging now."

"I've already noticed your hesitation." With two fingers, he stroked her back briefly and just perceptibly. "I am glad that you actually tell me."

She laughed merrily. "But of course. I don't want to put the slowfox at risk."

"Or the rumba with George." She hadn't even thought about it. Since she said nothing, he went on. "How long has it been since you last danced with your husband?

"Oh!" She recounted in thought the years since the accident. "An eternity. That was in another life."

"You've danced tournaments until your accident?"

"We did virtually nothing else. Except work, of course."

"Then this was really another life!" His gaze went to George. "I guess, after that he did the work on the board instead of the training." He looked at her attentively. "And you? In what did you find satisfaction instead?" Just why hadn't he shown so much empathy in dealing with Madeline? More and more she was amazed about him.

"I published two books on local dances in the Middle Ages.

Robert lost the beat. "You're a journalist or something?"

She laughed. "No, much worse. Historian. I have a professorship at the *Freie Universität*."

Robert swallowed, visibly impressed. For a moment his movements lost their lightness, but then he caught himself again.

She'd better not tell him that she had been the first woman ever to receive a senior professorship with her own chair in history. "Research saved me. At least that's what I could always do: read and write books."

He looked a little pensive. "One needs a hobby, so that the everyday life is not so gray. Dancing gives me the change I need."

She laughed. "So I was lucky twice. My hobby is also my profession. In a way."

Then this slow waltz came to an end, too. The conversation had distracted her so thoroughly that she had not been aware of the exertion. But now she was thankful that he linked arms with her when he accompanied her back to the table. By leaning on his arm, she could relieve her leg without visibly limping. Hopefully. The critical look that George took at her showed not only concern, but also open disapproval.

With a radiant smile for him she opened her dance card. "I'll dance the next dance with you." There were five other dances before this rumba. That should be enough to rest her aching leg. She hung her handbag over her shoulder. "I'm going to restore myself so I won't disgrace you." After a kiss on his cheek, she walked slowly to the exit of the hall. Five minutes of massage for her thigh away from George's watchful eyes; that was what she needed now.

The door to the small hall opened and for a moment disco music was roaring in her ears. The light in there flickered. Marga Fischer, who was actually only an office assistant, had once again spared no effort. But how did she manage to find a stroboscope? The Lietzensee Dance Club wouldn't be what it was if not for her. Even George called her the good spirit of the club; and that meant something, as he barely missed an opportunity to ascribe all the merit to himself.

Instead of hiding in the locker room to massage her leg, she could actually sit with Marga and chat with her. A bar stool was just as good.

Friederike turned to the bar. Her eyes widened in shock. Madeline hadn't gone home at all!

She had thought the girl in her bed. Instead, she sat in front of the bar on the floor, her head buried in the shoulder of a handsome man.

"Madeline!"

Madeline raised her head and blinked in surprise. The mascara had melted and her eyes were markedly reddened from crying.

"Grandma." A smile spread over her face.

Shock and indignation fought in Friederike. She eyed the man. "What are you doing there? Why did you cry?" It took her a moment longer, then she finally recognized him: Chris Rinehart, the caller of the square dancers.

"I didn't cry." Her voice wavered; was she drunk? Madeline looked at Chris. "Not really, anyway."

He helped her on her feet and stood too. Madeline hung on him like a sack of spuds. His face glowed just like that of Madeline. Did that mean the two had finally talked sense to each other?

Friederike walked up to them. She would have loved to

hug Madeline, but the girl obviously had a better support now.

"Hinnerk has me... has set me up." Madeline's voice squeaked before the rest of her words were strangled by a violent hiccup.

Friederike scrutinized Chris. "Are you just as drunk?"

"I can't afford that. I'll be on call tomorrow morning." He actually sounded sober; good. She didn't have to worry.

She sat next to them on a bar stool and started massaging her thigh. "I have something to tell you too, Madeline: I was dancing again!" She laughed at Madeline's stunned face.

The next moment Madeline had her arms around her neck and pressed her exuberantly to herself. She cried yet again. "Oh, Grandma, I'm so glad."

She sobbed and suddenly Friederike's eyes filled with tears too. "Then you shouldn't cry."

"Can I help you?" Chris interrupted her in a soft voice. He touched her kneading hand. "I can massage you. Loosen your cramped muscles if you don't want to go home and lie down."

"Home?" She laughed. "No, I'm going to enjoy this evening for a while longer."

Chris pushed her hand aside and set to work. He had obviously learned it like a real masseur.

Madeline wiped off her tears. "I'm so happy for you. How did Grandpa do?"

Friederike made a face. "I still have the first dance with your grandfather ahead of me. Your old friend Robert did the honors."

Madeline's mouth stood open. When she could close it again, she said: "I don't believe it. I just don't believe it."

"This is a night of miracles. Am I right, Chris?"

"That's how you can see it." With one hand he gently pulled Madeline towards him.

She turned to him and kissed him uninhibitedly. "A wonderful night."

Friederike slipped off the stool. "I don't want to miss this first dance with George. Take her home, Chris. Madeline belongs in bed."

Madeline pouted. "But..."

"Whichever one." She winked at the two of them. "Your grandfather thinks you've arrived there long ago anyway. Take care of her, Chris."

Rumba. She swung her hips once before she made her way back to the dance hall.

Robert had found another dance partner; so he had dared to. Werner Heinemann, the club treasurer, sat in Robert's place at their table. Judging by the worried face, engrossed in a serious conversation with George. Couldn't the man relax for once and stop counting the non-existent money?

The French pianist, Gaston or whatever his name was, began to play a milonga by Astor Piazzola. Many then left the dance floor; the milonga was not part of the official dance program. Still few in the club took the trouble to look outside the box: Ambition instead of fun was the main driving force, most notably for the Latin formation. And the tournament dancers even more! The Lietzensee Dance Club needed to understand that it had to be different from other dance clubs if it was to survive. Square dancing had been a good start, but actually nothing more than that.

No issue for now, though. She stepped behind Werner and put one hand on his back. "Where did you leave your wife?"

"I have no idea." His voice sounded even grumpier than usual. "She insisted that we come separately. And now I can't find her."

"Maybe she's at the disco with the kids?"

"Christina? Never!" He shook his head. "I'll just wait until the masks are lifted." Oh, that was it: He didn't know her costume at all.

She listened to the milonga, then she turned to George. "Next comes our rumba." She was truly thrilled. And she was even more pleased when he stood, buttoned his jacket and held out his arm for her. Just like old times. For so long she had thought she would never get to live it again.

"You're dancing, Friederike?" Shock and disbelief stood in Werner's face.

"You're astonished, aren't you?" She took George's arm and rose to a kiss on his cheek. "This is a night of miracles."

Werner sighed, obviously unable to share her happiness. "I could use one, too. For the club treasury. Or at least an affluent sponsor."

While walking, she grazed George as she moved her hips back and forth to loosen her pelvis for the rumba. Immediately he stopped, but when she smiled happily at him, he drew her closer to him. "Almost like old times."

He held her tighter than was proper for a rumba, but she wasn't sure of his reason and so she didn't want to say anything.

He lead her with forceful movements, as she had known him to do. But he was much stiffer than once; of course. After all those years in which he, too, had hardly danced. Previously with Robert she had moved in greater harmony. But it wasn't just that which made the unison difficult. After half a round in the hall she understood: In the first place George seemed anxious to recall the memory of her old step sequences and only secondarily cared that they had fun. His darn ambition. How often had he driven her to white hot with it, even though only by doing so did he lead them to their great achievements.

She stiffened involuntarily, but managed to bring about a smile for him. "It's just like old times!"

He stopped short and then he seemed to understand; he grinned back. "And like old times, you wait for ages, before you open your mouth." He stood still and got serious. "But one thing's different now. I don't want you exerting yourself." With his lips he fleetingly touched her cheek. "I'm too old to carry you on my hands."

His age had hardly been the reason for the distance in the last years, but that evening she didn't want to let bitterness arise. "Then I guess I'll need someone as young as this Robert. By the way, he really isn't a bad dancer at all."

George picked up the beat again and they kept dancing. "Madeline was stupid to dump him. She could have achieved a lot with him."

"We'll probably have to wait for our great-grandchildren to see tournament dancers in the family again."

"Then we won't see that at all!" He let go of her hip and sent her into a slow spin watching her facial expressions closely. "Isn't it too much for you, Rieke?"

"But no. It's all wonderful." She put her arms around his neck and pressed her face against his. "I feel like a young girl."

He frowned. "Nonetheless you don't have to act like one. We stand out."

"Old curmudgeon." She laughed. "Of course we stand out! How many of the club members here have ever seen us dance with each other?"

He looked around. "Nobody!" After the next spin he stopped and spoke to the couple whom they thus blocked the way. "You're surprised, aren't you?"

Those who had heard him laughed. And then the couples around them formed a circle. She held her breath for a moment. Actually it was appalling, but it could indeed contribute to George's reputation that the others saw him dance. Some of the young people might believe he could no longer do it.

When the dance ended, she was feeling her leg again; but for anything in the world would she have revealed that. She first beamed at the bystanders and waved as if she was back at a tournament; then she beamed at George. She hadn't seen him in such a good mood and relaxed for a long time. What could they possibly build on it!

2

On Monday morning Friederike still had trouble moving without constraint. Nevertheless, she inserted a CD and forced her aching limbs to obedience as she moved with swinging hips between the dining area, fridge and stove.

George sat at the breakfast table and kept an eagle eye on her movements as he had already done the whole Sunday. Finally, he seized her. "Looks like the ball sparked your spirits."

"I enjoyed it. I didn't realize how much I missed dancing."

"We had a good time together; I miss it sometimes too." He pulled her into the chair next to him. "But we also have a good life without our dance." Did he really think that? Then why did he spend most of his free time at the dance club? He stroked her back as if he had to appease her. "We can't turn back time. And we're not twenty anymore."

"You think I can't do this anymore!" Hadn't she proved to him often enough that she could do everything she wanted?

"Look how you torture yourself, Rieke!" He impatiently pressed his lips together. "That wasn't even half an hour. With long pauses in between. Two days ago!"

In one point, of course, he was right: It didn't work that way – yet. But she wanted to dance again and would get there, as she'd done with everything else after her accident. And with the dance, she'd get her marriage back. "Of course. The first time after... after sixteen years." She almost automatically put her hand on her leg. "That's not a muscle anymore. All cellulite."

"What?" In his gaze was perplexity.

"The great sorrow of all aging women: Wobbly flesh on the thighs."

The explanation made him look even more bewildered; so she preferred to end the conversation.

***

In the mid-morning Friederike sat in her office at the Friedrich-Meinecke Institute. When she got up from her computer to stretch, she moved with dance steps. At the faculty they were used to music playing in her office. Roberta Flaim, her secretary, would not notice that it was suddenly tango instead of minuet. But alone, of course, it wasn't the same as with a partner.

At noon Michael Hagwarth knocked on her door. The colleague, who was only a little older, researched Occitan music of the Middle Ages; together they worked on a research project on the origins of courtly dances of the Baroque.

Lost in thought, she massaged her thigh while he played on his laptop snippets of music that he had put together into a collage.

Suddenly he switched off in the middle of a piece of music. "What about your leg? Did you hurt it?"

Out of embarrassment, a heat wave shot into her face. "Oh, it's nothing."

"You overworked yourself." He looked at her just as skeptically as George had since the ball. "Doesn't anybody take care of you?"

"You know there's nothing stopping me."

"Certainly!" His gaze became even more alert than before. "And what have you done this time?"

She smiled; but different from George she didn't have to hide anything from him. Michael didn't wrap her in cotton wool. "I was dancing."

"Dancing?" His mouth stood open for a moment. Then he smiled. "Dancing is fine! And I thought you were interested in galliards and minuets purely scientifically."

"I need a dance partner, though!"

He stared at her in amazement. "What about your husband?"

"I didn't tell him I wanted to dance again."

"Rieke, Rieke!" He sat on the edge of her desk. "You deceive your husband? After so many years?"

She laughed amusedly. "After so many years, maybe it's time."

Michael looked shocked.

"I have no intention of deceiving him, as you call it. But a woman needs her little secrets. How else could we surprise you from time to time?"

"And why are you telling me this now?"

"Go dance with me." She turned on the music in her computer and moved to a pasodoble as best she could alone. The cha-cha-cha afterwards was easier in the demonstration. Then she stood still and looked at him expectantly.

He laughed quietly. "What was that? You want to convince me I'm not embarrassing myself with you?" He stood, counted one beat of the tango, which was playing in the meantime, and then took her in dancing position. "It's way too narrow in here," he said after three steps. "We have to go somewhere else." He still steered her into a promenade though. "But if you want to deceive your husband, I guess we can't go to his club. Or is there any chance we could stay there undetected?"

"I want to surprise him, not deceive him." She grinned mischievously. "If he discovers me in the dance circle, he'll be surprised too."

"And that's good?"

"George would never stoop to dancing in a dance circle." She shrugged. "That's almost like going to a beginner's class."

He looked at her suspiciously. "And you think that's good?" he repeated.

"I'll see." She laughed at his gloomy face. "What about it?"

"He might come up with the idea of beating me up."

"Then I'll protect you."

He grinned. "Are you strong enough?"

"I'm gonna enroll in a karate class at my gym."

"Then I dare. Just tell me when you've learned enough karate."

3

Friederike had let Madeline in on it and four weeks later she ventured into the Lietzensee Dance Club. Now it would show how much the additional training in her gym was worth.

"Family trip," Madeline announced to the astonished Marga Fischer when they entered the club rooms one hour before the start of the dance circle.

"Chris is tutoring you again?" Marga looked up from the crate of water bottles that she was emptying into the fridge behind the bar. "I thought you weren't doing that here anymore."

"Chris is on shift. He will again show up only at the last minute." She pushed Friederike closer to the bar. "Grandma's our private student today."

"But George is on the island of Rügen today and tomorrow to prepare for the North German Championships." Marga pulled a crate of beer in front of the open fridge door.

"Grandpa's not coming today. Exactly!" Madeline nodded. "She recruited a colleague from her department, and Hinnerk is coming too. He'll show them what Ines is doing right now."

Hinnerk Martens, Madeline's partner in square dancing, was also up to date in the dance circle, because he often helped out when a gentleman missed. That was why she had talked him into introducing Friederike and Michael to the current practice agenda of the dance circle.

Friederike didn't really know what to think of Margas countenance. But what was it to the office assistant? She had to register her membership and enroll her in the dance circle. And to give her a bottle of water afterwards.

"What does George say?" Marga was really curious.

"Can I get the key to the stereo?" Madeline seemed to have noticed Friederike's discomfort; she played chairman's granddaughter with this question.

Marga actually got distracted and went to the office to get it.

Friederike thankfully squeezed Madeline's hand.

Before Marga came back, Hinnerk looked around the corner. "No parking spots again." He grimaced. "I almost parked in Hong Kong."

"We don't have a helipad on the roof yet," Marga's voice came from behind him. She could be funny, too? That was comforting. – Marga held out the key to Madeline. "It's highly irregular."

"Why? The tournament couples also dance alone."

"Mrs. Lagrange isn't even a member of the club." Another disapproving look.

Friederike raised her eyebrows in bewilderment. What did Marga think she had to protect? "Why didn't you bring me a membership application? Wasn't it clear enough that I want to join the dance circle?"

Marga bent over the beer crate again. "We had stopped at the statement that George is on Rügen today."

"So what? I didn't know the chairman had to approve the admission applications."

Marga sighed and went back to the office.

"I don't know her like that," Madeline whispered. "What's the matter with her?"

Immediately afterwards Madeline received Michael like the mistress of the house, before Marga could bring out more than a "good evening". Love had obviously made her self-confident: And she had truly won a battle when she had stood up to George.

Madeline went to the office herself to get a second admission application. "For later! There's still something like a trial lesson."

Friederike laughed. "You know I don't need that."

"And what if it's too exhausting?" More and more, Marga made the impression that she wanted to keep her away.

"We can handle that," Michael declared. "I'm sure your coach won't rip our heads off if we extend the breaks on our own."

Marga shook her head. "What if everyone does?"

"Marga!" Madeline glared at her. "Now stop it. You sound like you don't want Grandma dancing. Should she look for another club?"

Hinnerk smirked. "What would George say to that?"

Madeline put her feet apart and lowered her voice as low as she could. "Rieke, you're damaging the reputation of our club." And then with her normal voice: "That means you're making me untenable as a board member."

Marga seemed shocked. "How do you talk about your grandfather?"

"Let it go, Marga. It's a family matter." Madeline took the key for the stereo and went to the small dance hall.

Friederike and Michael left the admission applications at the bar with Marga and followed Madeline. Hinnerk fetched se-ve-ral CDs from the cabinet in the hall; he played a slow waltz.

"Friederike, what steps do you still remember? Michael, how good are you at dancing?" Madeline leaned against the wall next to Hinnerk. "Show us. Then we let Hinnerk show what Ines last practiced in the dance circle."

Michael led Friederike into the middle of the parquet in a proper posture. Since mischief flashed in his eyes, she answered the tilting of his head with a curtsy, the just knee-length skirt gathered in her right hand. She already knew she'd have great fun.

He didn't hold her quite correctly; his hand was a little too deep in her back. But it didn't bother her: It felt like a well-intentioned support or as if he could lead her thus more easily. In fact, he placed his hand higher after a few steps. Along the first length of the hall he only danced the basic steps and she realized she hadn't asked him how well he could even dance. But it didn't really matter.

"How are you feeling, Friederike?"

"Everything's fine!" She beamed at him and pushed her hand a little higher to his shoulder; it was an automatic movement from her time with George. Only when he looked at her a little stunned did she notice. "Don't spare me, or you'll get bored." In truth, she herself began to find the movements monotonous. Suddenly she understood George's pretensions a little.

The next moment Michael surprised her with steps on the level of beginning tournament dancers. She went effortlessly with him and soon began to glow with zeal.

Michael stopped abruptly and put a hand on her cheek. "Are you okay?"

"Everything's fine!" she repeated. Probably she had hardly sounded convincing, because his gaze remained concerned. She pressed her face against his hand, which was still on her cheek. "You know I'm never pulling the wool over your eyes." With her hand on his shoulder, she pushed him into a movement.

He obeyed and they kept dancing. He repeated each figure twice before moving on to the next one. None of it was very exhausting – it was just a slow waltz. As the music faded, she knew the extra hours at the gym had paid off. Her thigh didn't twitch or throb. She put her hand unobtrusively on it. He felt cool under the fabric.

Hinnerk clapped his hands twice.

"Bravo," Madeline said. "Seems I missed something at the Carnival ball."

"You had more important things to do than watch me old lady." Relieved, she exhaled.

Michael must have watched her closely, because his eyebrows went up immediately.

She laughed, all relaxed. "I didn't gasp for air. That was a sigh of satisfaction."

He nodded. "I'd have been surprised otherwise. You certainly don't lack stamina."

"What's next, Hinnerk?"

"It's your choice, Grandma." Madeline held two CDs in front of her nose. "More standard or Latin? Both are current programs in the dance circle."

"I've always found Latin much more exciting." It matched her temperament and she liked the musics of Ravel and da Falla much better than those of Strauss and Gershwin.

Michael loosened his knees and then took two tango steps. "And how about this?"

She nodded; Piazolla was beautiful too... tango a good compromise. Although it counted among the Standards, it was as racy as the Latin American dances. Her breath became flat at the thought of stroking her leg along Michael's thigh.

"Tango it is!" Hinnerk put in the CD.

It was like a dream. Friederike danced most of the time with her eyes closed; she only opened them when Michael sent her into a movement from which she had to find her way back to him alone.

He stopped just before the end of the piece.

Surprised, she opened her eyes. "Everything's fine! It's okay."

"No!" His voice had a hard sound. "How long will you dance with me until your husband claims you?"

"That's what you think of me?" She choked out the words with difficulty, fighting sudden tears. "Do you really think I would just use you?"

"But that's what you want: To dance with George again to restore your marriage to its former glory."

She had a hard time denying that. It would be a lie and he would know it. "Gorge would never lower himself to dancing in a dance circle. He endures its existence gritting his teeth to nurture young talent for the club. The Lietzensee Dance Club doesn't have enough to offer to bait seasoned tournament dancers."

"And you want more than the dance circle, too."

Friederike shook her head. And that was the truth – as she saw it at the moment. "I'm just happy that I can venture back onto the floor." She looked at him pleadingly. "Can we talk about this later?"

He sighed and went with her to Madeline and Hinnerk.

"Now, let's take a look at Ines' current agenda. Agreed?" Madeline looked through the door at the clock above the bar. "We still have half an hour until the beginning."

"But we shouldn't dance until the last minute..." Michael looked at Friederike questioningly. "Ten minutes of tango, ten minutes of slow waltz." His gaze became insecure. "So you can have a short break."

"Don't worry! I don't mind you sentencing me to a break. You're right." She laughed as he apologetically raised his hands. "For once, for once."

And he was really right. After these twenty minutes she was more than happy to sit down and massage her thigh.

"Lack of training." She had Marga give her a mineral water. "And Michael secretly attached ten kilos of lead to my leg."

They had stopped just in time; shortly afterwards the first participants of the dance circle arrived. They greeted Madeline with blatant surprise. They were accustomed to Hinnerk standing in from time to time when a gentleman was missing.

But it was generally known that Madeline had found the love of her life with square dancing. In every way.

Then their surprise was even bigger when they learned that Friederike wanted to dance. And the whole time Marga was standing behind the bar with disapproving countenance.

When Ines Grube, the coach, called to begin, Friederike and Michael quickly filled in the applications.

"With this, I have sold my soul." Michael pushed his form over to Marga.

"For better or for worse!" For the first time that evening, Marga's face turned into a smile.

Hinnerk remained seated at the bar, but Madelinie walked next to Friederike when she went to the dance hall with Michael.

At the door she stopped Friederike and whispered in her ear: "You better call Grandpa and not wait until he comes back."

"Why is that?"

Madeline looked back towards the bar. "I'm sure you'd like him to hear it from yourself."

Michael followed her gaze. "I see!"

"What's 'I see'?"

"The woman at the bar has probably invested a few feelings too much."

"She's married!"

Michael raised his shoulders. "What difference does it make?"

Ines smiled over at them. "Tonight we have a new couple in our circle. I hope they will feel comfortable with us and stay: Friederike Lagrange and Michael Hagwarth. Some of you already know Friederike as the wife of our chairman. But most of you are too young to have witnessed her as a tournament dancer." She came up to Friederike and shook her hand. "Welcome back to our world."

"Thank you." Friederike swallowed hard.

Ines remained standing next to her, while she gave the instructions for the first dance. A new figure for the tango; but only slightly different from what Friederike had tried with Michael before. Confidently she let him go to the other side of the hall: At first the gentlemen had to practice alone what Ines showed them.

On Friederike's other side stood Tanja Walters, whom she had met as one of Madeline's friends. Tanja was actually a square dancer, but attended the dance circle for the sake of her younger brother Axel. She whispered in Friederike's ear. "Ines is a feminist in disguise. She torments the men until the step sits. Because we women can do it almost automatically if they lead us well."

Friederike's jaw dropped.

"Psst, don't tell anyone."

In fact, Ines then made the ladies do their footsteps alone only twice before letting them dance together. Ines' method was either effective or Michael an even more talented dancer than she had guessed.

After the tango came a slow waltz, but her leg hurt already. Nevertheless she did not want to end the fun and started the dance with her teeth clenched. But after three steps, Michael pulled her to the side. His gaze was a sole reproach.

"I don't want to stop yet!" She looked at him pleadingly. "Please!"

"Agreed. – If you allow yourself a ten-minute break now." He put his arm around her shoulders and nodded to Ines.

Quietly he opened the door and led her to the bar.

Madeline held her cell to Friederike. "I know you don't use one in your spare time. The Eight."

That distracted her for a moment from her frustration with Michael. "You have George on speed dial?"

Madeline shrugged. "After all, I'm a member of this club." She moved her head two centimeters in Marga's direction, which stood bent over in front of the fridge and emptied bottles into the lowest compartment. This gesture was probably supposed to mean there was a haste to call George.

Friederike still did not want to believe it. Marga had a reputation for being helpful and caring. It was said, without her the daily routine of the club would run only half as smoothly. However, it had been obvious earlier that she felt called to interfere.

Michael presented her with a small bottle of Prosecco. "That or a water?"

"Water; I'm thirsty."

Madeline took the Prosecco for herself and bent over the bar for a glass. "Marga, would you push over a fizz for Grand... for Friederike?" She grinned at Friederike. "You're not old enough to wear this title in public."

Michael laughed heartily. "There you're saying some truth!"

Marga brought her the water. She drank while listening to the dial tone on the cell. Then the voicemail started. "George is not available now." So there was also no danger of Marga reaching him.

She slipped from her stool and moved her left leg sideways and backwards for a test. It could go on. "Everything's fine!" How many times did she actually say that on this night? She linked arms with Michael.

"The next time you take a break, you'll have to do without me," Madeline said. "Should I leave my cell here at the bar for you?"

"Friederike can use mine." Michael took a look at Marga. "If it's really that urgent."

In the meantime Ines had gotten to slowfox.

After one dance a throbbing pain became palpable in Friederike's thigh, but she managed to stay relaxed next to Michael, so that he didn't notice anything. She practiced the next steps with him; it was all so familiar. If only her leg could hold out, it wouldn't be a problem at all to dance again. – Exercise; she needed a few months of exercise to get the muscles strong again.

Then Ines went to the stereo and turned on the music.

Friederike stopped Michael. "I'd like to skip that now."

He nodded. "I should have known I could trust you."

This time he first exchanged a few words with Ines before leaving the hall with her.

Hinnerk wasn't sitting at the bar anymore; neither Madeline of course. The door to the great hall was now closed; muffled country music came out.

"Water?"

Friederike shook her head.

"Cell?"

She hesitated. Actually it should seem strange to George if she called directly from the club now. Just like that, without any pressing reason.

Michael involved Marga in a conversation by questioning her about her work and then about the groups that currently were dancing in the club. Of course, she succumbed to his charm within five minutes. That had already been clear to Friederike the moment she had reacted with an absurdity to Michael's stupid line. Several times she even laughed out loud.

Marga absorbed every word of recognition like a sponge. Suddenly Friederike believed Michael's assumption that Marga had a little – or even a little more – crush on George. George, like Michael, knew how to wrap people around his finger. Hence he had been the undisputed chairman and figurehead of the Lietzensee Dance Club for so many years. Of course also because it was not necessarily a job that everyone wanted to do. Who, like George, was ready to be there for the club virtually day and night? Besides Marga?

Marga was just as committed as George: At any rate, what she told Michael sounded like it. It also matched the remarks Friederike had occasionally picked up about her.

Indeed, she'd better call George right away. Maybe Marga used to report to him at the end of the evening. And if she then lost a word about her presence...

Friederike reached out to Michael. "Cell, please."

He fished it out of his trouser pocket and held it to her as he continued the conversation with Marga. Then he even leaned over the counter: distraction maneuver. She should be able to make a call without Marga eavesdropping.

Still, she walked a few steps away from the bar before dialing George's cell number.

This time he accepted the call right after the first ring tone. In the background there was a television; so the session was over.

"Good evening, George!"

"Rieke! Well, that's nice of you to call. The session ended five minutes ago and I just opened a wine from the mini-bar."

She listened for the background noises: no voices. He wasn't distracted. The TV, at best.

"Wait a minute." The TV went silent. Then he began to talk about the meeting; in his enthusiasm he showered her with a torrent of words. If she didn't interrupt him now, she wouldn't get to dance again.

She held up the cell to capture some of the dance music that quietly penetrated through the upholstered doors of the halls to the bar.

At that he paused; a noise told her he was changing his position. "Where are you, Rieke?"

"You wouldn't guess." She made him hear her smile.

"At the club? Did you take Madeline to her group?"

"At the club; right. But vice versa, Madeline escorted me to my group."

Slowly, amazement came into George's voice. "Your group." He cleared his throat. "Dance circle. You're really serious, Rieke?"

"Didn't you think I could do this?"

"I trust you to do anything, *chérie.*" Again he changed position; his voice lost some of its warm sound. "Rieke, don't make yourself miserable. After that, you can't walk for weeks again."

"I dance, I don't walk. I appreciate your concern; you know that. But stop wrapping me in cotton wool. That doesn't agree with me."

"Rieke!" What was that supposed to mean? He didn't seem happy. It almost sounded like he didn't approve. "And who are you dancing with?"

"Michael Hagwarth from the Department of Medieval History."

"Who?"

"My colleague in the project 'Dance'."

"So you've been lucky." But he didn't sound like that. More like he was piqued that she had found someone willing to dance with her.

"He's waiting." She quickly ended the conversation with the question of when he would be home again.

When she closed the cell and turned around, she crossed Marga's gaze. Probably it had indeed been wise to call him before Marga told him she was dancing.

She hated that. There was enough intrigue in the faculty; she didn't have to have it here, too. This was the main reason why she had stayed away from the dance club; not the regret about her lost dance career.

Ines ended the evening with a cha-cha-cha and Friederike was rested enough to let Michael lead her on the floor again.

When she came home then, she limped and had to lean on the railing to get up the stairs. But for nothing in the world

would she have taken the elevator. How good that George
was on Rügen.

4

The next morning Friederike was dragging herself through the house with aching legs: sore muscles. Her thigh was also very unpleasant, but the sore muscles prevailed. She was downright happy with it, since it was a little like old times.

She prepared a hot bath, took her coffee and her e-book reader and made herself comfortable in the tub all morning long. Afterwards she felt better, but she would certainly need the next two days to banish the sore muscles completely. Hopefully Michael would be creeping around on Monday as much as she was.

George didn't come back until late in the night. She had taken a hot shower and then settled down with a wine in front of the late night movie. He watched her again with an eagle eye as she stood to fetch the wine bottle from the kitchen.

She poured and held the glass out to him. "I'm aching like old times."

"That probably means you've put up with too much, like old times." As if it hadn't always been him who was pushing them. But unlike before, his gaze now expressed disapproval, not appreciation for her effort.

She sat next to him on the sofa and pulled her legs up. "I didn't know there were a couple more muscles I should have been training in the last few weeks. I was just thinking about the thigh."

George put his hand on it; then on the other one and back again. "It seems to me that it's a little warm."

"Not warm enough." She shoved his hand a little higher and pressed herself closer to him. "I need you to care for me, not to worry." She unbuttoned his shirt and put her hand on his naked chest. "You were gone almost two days."

"Now I'm supposed to catch up." He laughed throatily. "Do you think I can make it up to you?"

"Maybe if you start right now..."

"You could have come with me. Leave me to myself two nights in a cold bed, that wasn't nice of you."

"Then I'll have something to make up for as well." She nibbled on his neck. "An eye for an eye?"

He pushed the dressing gown off her shoulder. "Bite for bite..." And that was the end of the conversation for the evening.

This was almost the only thing that hadn't changed in the many years of her marriage. George was a great lover, though insatiable. Sometimes she wondered if he would have stayed with her if the accident had taken that away from them, too. But she had no reason to doubt his faithfulness. He had not even looked for a new dance partner, although she had expressly encouraged him to do so. And a woman like Marga couldn't hold a candle to her. If the woman even danced?

At breakfast George went on and on reporting about the tournament preparations on Rügen. He was convinced that at least one of the two couples of the Lietzensee Dance Club had a good chance to reach the top places. "Melanie Sturmann would have had one, too. But now she's changed partners twice in a short time. That never works." He beheaded his egg. "I do know why I didn't even try back then."

"You can practice dance as a sport even without tournaments. Balance for the body. Burn the excess adrenaline."

"It's not the same." George made a face, and in a moment he would scornfully lower the corners of his mouth. "I'm not suffering from excess adrenaline." She was careful not to contradict that.

"Ambition isn't everything." Sometimes she'd hated his ambition. Another half hour of practice and another half hour and another... She'd gone home far too tired far too often. The other driver was to blame for the accident; but if she hadn't been so tired, she could have reacted faster, and then, who knew...

George suddenly stood next to her and lifted her chin. "Come back, Rieke." He smiled, but there was concern in his eyes. He was always afraid she'd overexert herself. "Will you go back to the dance circle next Friday?"

Why did he ask that? He hopefully didn't want to... "That's the plan." Michael had gotten her word; she certainly wouldn't break it. "We've both signed up for the club." She let her eyes participate in her smile. "So I won't be in any doubt in the first place."

"Or your dance partner."

"Oh he... He'll probably doubt a lot: the wisdom of his decision." But she didn't believe what she said. Michael wasn't like that. "He's got to make a lot allowances – compromising before I'm ready to dance through a full evening."

"Be careful, Rieke."

"I am. This is fun; true pastime without any purpose."

George raised his eyebrows.

"Except, of course, for the purpose of enjoying the dancing – finally floating again." She smiled at him. "No matter how far I get with this. After all, at my age..."

"At our age, *chérie*! I haven't gotten any younger either. And some things should be left to the really young ones."

"Why did you ask whether I'm going back to the dance circle on Friday?"

He stroked her hair. How she hated that gesture. "Because then I'd better stay home. What would it look like if I was standing next to you? Like I'm guarding my wife."

"As you already had to watch out for Madeline."

"And that went promptly wrong."

"You mean it was unsuccessful."

"No, I mean 'went wrong'. You'll see, that ends with a great tragedy. Your granddaughter knows no bounds; she knows only drama."

"Chris is a good man."

"All the worse. When she's in the prime of her life, he'll be ripe for retirement."

That was just typical; he couldn't take any defeat. How did they actually survive the shared failures?

She refrained from the remark that the age difference between the two of them was virtually as big as that between Chris and Madeline.

5

Despite the hot baths and George's massages, Friederike's muscle ache was in full bloom on Monday. As she climbed the stairs to her office in the faculty, she first met Thomas Immenfels, the head of the faculty: Very worried, he stopped her and asked if something had happened to her leg. Then Roberta came up the stairs behind her and stopped in shock. After that Friederike decided that she would not leave her office until closing time.

At the end of the morning Michael came prancing into her office, really and truly prancing.

"Have you recovered, Rieke?" He gave her a kiss on the cheek. "What I've heard during the morning..." He laughed, so he didn't take it seriously.

"My muscle ache is a full-grown tiger." She shrugged.

"And your leg? Is it all right?"

"Everything's fine!"

They laughed at the line: their new running gag.

"You, on the other hand, I see you've been practicing secretly for the last few weeks. I almost thought so when I saw how well you were dancing on Friday."

"I couldn't have let you down... after you told me about your Carnival ball with those smiling eyes." He pushed a stack of papers aside and sat next to her on the desk. "I know you; don't you know that?"

"I do!" But didn't Michael then have to believe that she wouldn't trade him for George in the dance circle?

"And knowing that you did not want to take the first steps with your unruly husband..."

"He really is a little..." Nervously she began to sort the papers Michael had pushed together. "He worries all the time; sure. But I thought he'd be more excited."

"Then it's probably a good thing you called him right away."

She nodded. "He asked if we'd go back to the dance circle next Friday."

"Obviously, he's really not enthusiastic."

"You're thinking the same I was thinking. But it's quite different: He wants to avoid showing up at the same time as me. He usually spends every Friday night at the club." She smiled. "George is always good for a surprise."

"Well. But that's not why I came. Not even because someone here worries." Michael got off her desk and opened his briefcase. "It's because someone seems envious." He held a thin folder in her face. "You don't have a copy, do you?"

"What's that?" She took the folder and opened it. It was a *"Call for Papers"* from Oxford University, Faculty of Music: The Music Faculty of the venerable English University was planning a conference for autumn and invited to submit topics.

"Why don't I have it? How did you get this?"

"By chance. Tom spoke to me about your lame gait and asked if that was the reason he hadn't received a proposal from you yet." He growled. "Of course, I was sure you would have told me. So I had no qualms about claiming you knew nothing."

She began to read the *Call for Papers* more closely. "My goodness! It's almost closing date."

"That's why Tom asked. From Carlsen he's got the proposal a week ago; and since now it has to be decided whose travel expenses will be covered..."

"Carlsen!" The man was more on the road than in his lectures.

"Tom's secretary is behind it."

She stared at him in shock.

"Karin reacted strangely when he asked her to make another copy for you. And when he asked when she had sent you the first one, he got no answer."

"She's involved with Carlsen."

"For that, she's going so far as to embezzle the mail to you?" Now it was Michael who looked shocked. "Carlsen is married!"

Friederike was boiling with rage; but she managed well enough to appear unmoved on the outside. "You know well, how important the Oxford Conferences are."

"It could cost her her job."

"Which she won't need anymore if he marries her."

He laughed contemptuously. "Carlsen won't divorce for anybody. More than one has tried that."

"Oh, you men! You know that about each other and leave us in the dark?"

"The usual... locker gossip. What a man boasts about after a weekend."

He sat back on her desk. "Do you need my help to get this proposal done in time?"

She continued to leaf through the *Call*, reading individual paragraphs more closely. "Write a page about your part of our project for me. Till Friday."

"And right away it's about to cost us the dance circle."

"But no. Stupid! You give me your page in the afternoon and after the course we go to the pub and discuss it. And if I just strain my leg and not my head, I'll be able to finish everything over the weekend." She grinned. "Actually, it's just like old times: Squeezing dance dates between the work... No, the other way round; squeezing the work between dance dates."

"That must have been pretty hard sometimes."

"But dancing has never fallen short." She smiled at him. "It won't now either."

But Michael didn't return her smile. "You didn't have your professorship back then."

"No." He kept looking at her, waiting for more than that. "And without the accident, I probably never would have gotten it." In the endless first months, when she could hardly move, she had had nothing but books to kill time. And all the scientific journals George had brought her almost daily had helped her to specialize. Enough to apply for a chair as soon as she could move in a wheelchair.

At that time she had made friends in the faculty: people who admired her for her toughness. And a few enemies like Carlsen, who said she had gotten the place he had been entitled to with the help of the Disabled Persons Act. And then, when she was recovering more and more... The day she entered the faculty on foot for the first time, he had looked at her as if he wanted to throw her down the stairs.

And now Tom's secretary had tried to oust her. The way she knew Carlsen, he had already sent in his paper; convinced that he was now the only one who would apply for travel expenses. But her paper would be the better one – Tom had a good reason to ask Michael: He wanted her project to represent the Institute's ongoing work. Carlsen would have to go to Oxford at his own expenses or would have to renounce.

After Michael left, she went to work. First she sketched a summary for her lecture; then she called Tom's office to discuss the proposal with him. She didn't have time for a second version: The first draft had to meet his expectations right away so that he could stand behind her travel expenses application in the faculty council without any ifs or buts.

To her surprise, a strange voice answered her in Tom's

secretariat to put her through. Tom then told her straight away that his secretary had been put on leave.

Friederike swallowed. Karin was a nice girl. Actually, she didn't deserve to lose her job because of this unfortunate affair. But she said nothing; she was not other people's keeper.

Instead, she asked Tom for his opinion on her intended contribution. He surprised her once again, because he suggested that Michael's part of the project should be more prominent and that she take him to Oxford. At the expenses of the faculty, of course.

Of course she agreed. It was a great opportunity for Michael to make a name for himself. She was yet other people's keeper. Sometimes.

Afterwards she had a lot of trouble to gently inform Michael they might have to cancel the dance circle after all, because his contribution should be more detailed than expected.

"Night shift," was Michael's comment. "We can do both."

She was careful not to tell him anything about priorities and choices in life. He was an adult. When she thought hard, she sometimes even remembered that he was older than she was.

"Night shift!" Thursday morning Michael came into her office with his eyes reddened with fatigue. He had not only written his part for the paper; he had also compiled music examples and loaded them into his dropbox, to which he linked in the manuscript.

Thursday evening he came home to Friederike and after dinner in threes they left George for his football reports and sat in her study to the final version for Tom. Another night shift.

But Friday night they went to the dance circle.

A week later, the faculty council approved the travel expenses for both of them. Carlsen fumed and Karin had an entry in her personnel file which could lead to a dismissal at the next offense.

Carlsen had actually already submitted his paper. Yet he did not withdraw it, but was obviously willing to participate at his own expense.

6

For five months Friederike went regularly to the dance circle with Michael. The first Friday they were missing was the day they flew to the Oxford conference.

On the penultimate day of the conference week, the Mayor of Oxford gave a reception and a ball. At first Friederike danced only with Michael and refused the requests of others. But soon it made an odd impression even on herself. In the end she even ignored the warnings from her thigh and left out only a few dances.

Like the whole week, the BBC was present that evening with a team. But these weren't science journalists, now people from the local newsroom produced the footage. In a few weeks time the city council elections were on the agenda and the mayor was looking for the limelight.

But the secret star of the evening was Friederike. She only found out when a camera kept her persistently in the view-finder after dancing with the mayor.

"And this to me! Of all things." Yet it amused her more than it bothered her.

Michael turned his head in all directions, as if he had to study the guests. "There's no one here that would be a more attractive subject. Besides, apart from the significant others, there are almost no ladies among the conference participants anyway." He grinned. "The power to interpret history is still firmly in the hands of men."

"Only it won't do you much good anymore."

"Since we have traitors among us like the wise Monsieur Duby. But he also betrayed you feminists."

She laughed. "I'm a feminist?"

"Sure thing. Otherwise, you never would have become a professor. You would have backed down, like the other women in the faculty, impressed by the power of the male mind."

"You're lucky I'm not a traitor. If your female students find out what you just said."

Michael looked at the cameraman, who stood only a few steps away. He lowered his voice. "Do you think he recorded our conversation?"

She turned around. He actually seemed to still have her in his viewfinder. "Whatever. It's just local TV. And the anchors don't understand German anyway. If not even the ones from 'Science' speak foreign languages."

"Not that they're posting it on the Internet."

"Just don't give your seminar tasks during which research could lead to discovery."

"In other words: I'm supposed to hide my light under a bushel. Is that the kind of advice that ousted your competitors?"

Friederike laughed. "I can do even a lot better."

"I'd rather not know that exactly now. You better dance with me again if you can."

"I can." And if she had to be carried on the plane tomorrow: This was her first dance in the wild. She'd enjoy it till the last minute.

But she was tired. Like all conferences, this one, too, had brought her to the brink of exhaustion. Too much talk, too little sleep. Too much food, too little coffee.

She leaned her head against Michael's shoulder and let the music carry her along. Blues or rumba; she didn't care anymore. And she had nothing against it, when soon after he put his arms around her neck and pulled her closer to himself.

"You're a great partner, Friederike," he whispered in her ear. His mouth obviously was only millimeters from her neck. Suddenly, his remark seemed ambiguous. As if he didn't mean their cooperation. Or not only.

She did not dare to inquire; would not destroy the magic of the evening. But maybe it was wrong. Maybe that was what she needed to do right now. She exhaled heavily and the thumb in her neck stroked her.

"Does it strain you too much?"

"I want to keep dancing, keep dancing..."

It was two o'clock in the morning when she wished him a good night outside the door of her hotel room.

With a sudden sense of guilt, she remembered she hadn't called George. But now it was too late and the following evening she would be home anyway. To soothe her conscience, she sent him a text message before she turned off the light.

7

George picked her up at the airport. "How tired are you?" he asked after she said goodbye to Michael.

"Like every time." She suppressed a yawn. "This morning I didn't get to bed until two and I had to go to breakfast at half past six."

He laughed. "I know! I saw your message."

"Oh?" She'd forgotten all about it by now. "Did I wake you up with it?"

"But no. I've tossed and turned sleepless, yearning for you."

She frowned for a moment. What kind of line was that? "Basically, we could save ourselves these conferences these days. It's all on the Internet anyway, and we can discuss also on Skype."

"But careers still function as they did in the Stone Age: through personal contacts and old boy networks."

"That's right." She proudly told of Michael's successful lecture and the invitations he had received afterwards. Suddenly she was all awake again.

"You care a lot about him!" That sounded a little disapproving.

She looked at him in astonishment. "He's the brightest head I've had as a colleague in a long time. And on top of that, reliable. What you can't often say especially about the smartest."

"And he's dancing with you!" That now was clearly disapproving.

She shrugged. "I guess he's happy to have found a partner who's not so demanding." Hopefully she had phrased this neutrally enough that he did not feel criticized. But even without her saying so, he knew of course she had asked Michael because George would never have gone to the dance circle with her like a lousy beginner. "Why did you ask how tired I am?"

"We could stop by Bruno's house."

"I'd like that, yes." She smiled. "If necessary, I can sleep on the sofa until you find an end." That would be a surefire distraction from this sensitive subject.

George, of course, had expected them to go to Bruno's. Konstanze, her enchanting daughter-in-law, and Chris stood in the kitchen between food preparations like for a party: desserts and *hors d'oeuvres* on the worktop next to the fridge, roast and *gratin dauphinois* in the oven, a large pot of *ratatouille* on the stove and three different salads on the table.

George looked at Chris with blatant aversion. "Where's Madeline?"

"She's cramming." Like a trained waiter, Chris took three *hors d'oeuvres* over his arm and opened the kitchen door with his foot.

Konstanze held out two salad bowls to George. "Take these to the dining room, will you?"

He looked at Friederike. "Well, actually..."

Konstanze went even closer with the bowls and held them directly under his nose. "You'll have her the rest of the night. It's girl's time now."

He growled and left with the bowls.

Konstanze poured a coffee and handed it to Friederike. "Sit down! You must be tired."

They made the men wait until the roast was ready, while Friederike was talking. Konstanze laughed gloatingly when she told her about Carlsen's efforts to make an impression.

But when she then spoke of Michael's lecture and of the recognition he had reaped for it, Konstanze frowned and her eyes got a worried expression. "What kind of guy is he, this Michael?"

Friederike laughed quietly. "You ask the same question as George did!"

Konstanze reached for the thermal gloves. "George is worried about one of your colleagues? I didn't imagine he would do such a thing."

"Probably because he's my dance partner, too."

Konstanze let go of the handle of the oven door and turned to her. "That's him?" She whistled through her teeth; Friederike hadn't even known that she could that. "I saw you on TV."

"You did what?" Shocked, she widened her eyes.

"A part of the science show this morning." Konstanze turned back to the oven. "You danced." It sounded casual, but her tense shoulders revealed she saw a problem in it. Carefully she took out the roast and put the pot on the table.

"And what makes you think it was Michael they showed me off with?" Surely her dance with the mayor had rather been cut into the finished feature.

"George also saw the contribution. He was not amused." Konstanze placed the roast on a serving plate and poured the sauce into a small pot, which she put on the stove to thicken. "It was a sight indeed!"

Was that why George had been so weird earlier? "What do you think of me?" Friederike herself was not convinced of the indignation she put into her voice.

Konstanze gave her a look from the side as she seemed to concentrate on stirring the cream into the sauce. "That you enjoyed being treated as a desirable woman. George hasn't done it the way he's supposed to for a long time."

"But Konstanze! He loves me!"

"So!" Suddenly George's grim voice sounded from the door.

Startled, Friederike drove around.

Konstanze stopped stirring. "Isn't it true? Don't you love Friederike anymore?"

George's eyes were angry slits. "You didn't speak of me."

"We did!" Konstanze sounded pissed off.

"Not only." Friederike smiled tenderly at him. "I told about Oxford."

"Exactly!"

Valiantly she maintained her smile. "Konstanze told me that the science show had provided a lengthy contribution about it. You saw it too, she says." Konstanze had finished with the sauce; Friederike stood and took the plate with the roast. "You didn't tell me anything about that."

"What for? You were there, weren't you?" His voice was still grim.

She pushed the door open with her elbow. "But I'm interested to know they had a segment about the conference in the first place. That they see it important enough..."

She left him there and went into the living room. George was upset. How could he? If only she knew what had been shown of the ball.

Chris took the roast from her. "I'll get Madeline."

Bruno looked at her with raised eyebrows. "What's the matter, Mother?"

"Nothing." She laughed nervously. He didn't believe her. She wouldn't be surprised if George had talked to him about the show. Certainly Bruno had noticed then that George... yes, what... was jealous? And that at their age. Ridiculous!

Madeline saved her for the moment. She rushed towards her and spun her around. "Grandma, I heard you had a great success." She gave Chris a conspiratorial look. "Finally someone's interested in the old dances."

Chris burst out laughing. "Madeline has set her mind on making our troupe dance the quadrille."

Madeline turned to him and put her hands on her hips. "And why shouldn't we? Then we'd have an advantage over the other square dance groups. Grandma can teach us; she's researched it long enough."

"Yes, I would like that. We could borrow the ancient outfits from the opera's pool."

Chris snorted, but the laughter lines around his eyes betrayed him: He wasn't serious. "When the club then doesn't need me anymore, George finally has a real reason to kick me out."

"Never." Madeline reached for him. "He won't dare to do that again. He knows we'd all go then." She kissed him uninhibitedly first on the cheek, then on the mouth and deepened her kiss until he put her arms around her.

George came from the kitchen, the pot with *ratatouille* in his hand, and Konstanze followed with *gratin dauphinois*. For a moment there was uncomfortable silence in the room. Then Bruno broke the ice with the question who to pour from the *Tressallier* he had opened for the *hors d'oeuvres*.

Madeline asked about the Latin tournament in Bremen and George instantly forgot everything else. He proudly reported how the club's formation had fought its way to the top. "And next year, we'll let them go to the World Championships."

"And who's gonna pay for that, Dad?" Bruno did not seem to understand that Madeline's question had been a diversion. The girl wasn't interested in the formation at all.

George George straightened himself. "The club has still mastered all financial challenges. We'll just have another open house day and a tombola." He was looking around like he was the one organizing such an event. "The last one was a great success."

"All right, Grandpa! Let's have another open house day. It was fun for everyone." Madeline gave Friederike a conspiratorial look. "This time, we're truly taking time with the preparations. Then we'll get to put together something really special."

Chris pinched her in the arm. "Darling, don't you dare."

Madeline fluttered her eyelids innocently. The way the two looked at each other, it was quite unthinkable that George was right with his doom and gloom prophecy. They simply matched perfectly... But she and George had also been a perfect match once. And then the accident had ruined all their plans.

In the course of the meal, the conversation naturally ended up at her conference again; especially Madeline was burning with curiosity. She seemed to be seriously interested in giving the courtly dances of the Baroque again a performance. At times she even swept George along with her zeal.

But they weren't talking about the TV show. George didn't come back to it either when they finally got home.

He put her suitcase in the hallway. "I suppose most of it goes to the laundry room."

She nodded.

"I'll do it for you. You must be tired." Of course it meant, "and you shouldn't climb stairs unnecessarily".

"You mean I have to go to bed now?" She kissed him gently. "I'm always glad to come home." George didn't react, so she put her arms around his neck. "Yes, I think I'll go to bed now."

He stood stiff and tense and made no move to return her embrace. Sighing, she pushed the elevator button.

8

Of course, colleagues from the faculty had also seen the science magazine and one of them had had the presence of mind to press the record button of his video recorder. Roberta proudly brought Friederike a copy.

The show focused on the lectures of the German participants: hers, Michael's and Carlsen's. These were all takeovers from the BBC. There was also a footage from the final reception at Oxford Mayor's - and it showed a moment during the ball when she had leaned her tired head against Michael's shoulder. After George's reaction she had feared something like this.

How embarrassing; she could only... pray that the colleagues would overlook these pictures. But that would probably be in vain.

However, the report of the science magazine went even further. With an own contribution by the German team of journalists: an interview with Carlsen. The professor, of course – machos all of them. Friederike clenched her fists furiously.

She didn't have to do that to herself. She got up to turn off the VCR. At that moment, Carlsen said, "Of course, we've got at the faculty..." We at the faculty? The guy had the gall to present himself as the representative of the faculty?

"Roberta!" Friederike gasped. "Did you see that? What does Tom say?"

Roberta shrugged. "What do you want him to do?" Of course, Tom couldn't do anything. They couldn't dismiss a professor with civil servant status; and as long as he did not steal silver spoons... She went to her office and called Michael.

In her anger, she had forgotten that he was having a seminar. With an exasperated growl she sat at the computer and began to rewrite and add to her conference contribution to turn it into a chapter for the intended publication.

Then came Michael, in a good mood as always. Didn't he know anything yet?

"I want you in my book. How much time can you spare in the next few weeks?" Carlsen would not shy away from integrating their work in some way into his own publication if they did not publish first. She had no nerve wasting her time on a plagiarism discussion.

"You sound like you're in a sudden hurry." Michael laughed. "You already have your professorship."

"But you haven't, Michael." She didn't want to laugh along. "Did you see the magazine segment?"

"No. But I've heard of it. I should probably take a look." He blushed suddenly. "I've been mightily teased this morning. We were obviously filmed while dancing." He grinned again. "I'm sure you'll hear it too: Rainer Weidner now attributes the power of miraculous healing to me because I made you dance again."

"And that was all the colleagues cared about?" She looked at him in disbelief and dismay.

He shrugged. "Finally something to gossip about. We haven't had it for a long time."

"The Messrs science journalists interviewed Professor Carlsen." She snorted in outrage.

Michael still shrugged.

"And he had the audacity to act as the official representative of the faculty."

"Well. In the conference documents he was named as one of the delegates. Why would he enlighten them?" Of course that was a point – and the reason why Tom's hands were tied. He wouldn't upset the organizers at Oxford.

"Whatever. That's why I want to publish quickly now."

"We're better than Carlsen." Michael grinned. "Our book will definitely be unbeatable."

She shook her head. "If his comes out first, he'll still get the reviews and the mentions. You know that very well. Nobody cares two hoots about the next book on a similar subject."

"Agreed. We're done first. Make the contract and get a deadline from the publisher." He sat on the edge of the desk and played with her fountain pen. "And if we make it by then, we'll include a CD with the book. If not, we'll publish it separately."

"A CD!"

"One of my friends has a studio and professional recording equipment."

"Why new recordings? You've already cut together the right music examples for Oxford; and I have more. Or we could just mention them in the sources." She took away the fountain pen; George had given it to her twenty years ago. "Many a musician will be delighted. But Carlsen will do the same."

A mischievous grin spread across his face. "But he won't have any danced examples." He tapped her on the nose. "What do we have... our dance club for?"

Oh! What an idea! She burst out laughing. "Madeline would be terribly pleased. She just suggested on the weekend to rehearse a quadrille for the next open house day. If we can get Chris to do it."

"If not, I'll play the dance master." Michael began to sort her felt-tip pens.

"The square dancers won't go along with that. They'd smell rubbish again." Friederike told him what George had instigated when Madeline fell in love with the caller of the group. And how the group had threatened to leave the club because they didn't want to give up Chris.

Michael was more and more shocked the longer she spoke. She'd never seen him beside himself like that before. "I wouldn't have thought your husband capable of that."

"He meant well."

"What?" He seemed to lack words.

She better not shock him any more. He'd have to get along with George if they wanted to make his idea a reality. They needed the approval of the board and probably also something from the budget of the club. Of course, they could finance the borrowing of the costumes with their research funds. But that would hardly go unnoticed by Carlsen, even without the secretary Tom had removed from his office. And she didn't want to risk him copying the idea. These laurels belonged to Michael. All alone to him.

Michael slowly regained his composure. "Yeah, sure; sometimes we think we know better what's good for others." He seemed hesitant to say any more. "And I guess your husband's one of those who think that a lot." His insecurity was tangible.

With a laugh she tried to dispel the tension that suddenly stood in the room. "Don't worry, Michael. You can just say what I think." She tapped on her screen. "But let's get to the point. I need four weeks to get my chapters together." She smiled mischievously. "Without skipping the dance circle."

"On the contrary. We're gonna make our movie appealing to them, too. You'll see."

The following Friday Friederike and Michael stopped at the bar after the dance circle. As they had agreed before, Michael took the lead. "I've heard there's going to be another open house day." He gave Marga a smile while she filled his wine glass. "Are you planning it again?"

She put the bottle away. "Nothing has been decided yet. And I hadn't even planned it, just suggested. The formation did the work."

Michael turned his glass between his fingers. "Once I'd like to see them dance."

"You're in the mood for Latin, Michael?" Werner Heinemann put his beer down and turned all his attention to him. "There's a dancer looking for a new partner right now."

Michael laughed. "The formation's that bad?"

Marga dropped her jaw.

"Well, if they'd take a guy like me, they can't be good."

"You don't dance that bad, Michael," came the voice of Ines from behind. "You'd have to practice more; that's all."

"Well... Some people can reconcile work and dancing." Michael nodded in Friederike's direction. "Did you see that report in the science show the other day?" He looked around questioningly. "Rieke's research is ideal for this."

Werner frowned. "Indeed? Last I heard, you were dealing with some ancient dances. Not anymore?"

Friederike held out her wine glass to Marga for refilling. "Not that old. At least not so much older than the waltz."

Tanja Walters made a skeptical face. "And what do you mean by that? Three hundred years instead of two hundred?"

"Sort of. Mozart, for example, also wrote minuets."

"Were they for dancing?" asked Werner's wife Christina.

Friederike nodded. "Of course. The Baroque suites are a series of dances."

"For dancing", Michael added with a broad smile. "What else for?"

"To listen. I've heard that these house musics stretched over hours and hours. If I imagine that..." Tanja yawned demonstratively. "I fall asleep when concerts last more than an hour."

"You see, we'd better dance these." Axel, her brother, pushed her in her side.

"But the house musics..."

"House musics, that was the bourgeoisie, Tanja. People who didn't have castles and ballrooms and therefore no place to dance." Axel grinned. "But actually, the music back then was commissioned by kings or something." The two were getting tangled up in their usual banter.

Suddenly Tanja shot her index finger at Friederike. "Madeline tries to talk Chris into rehearsing a quadrille for the next open house day." She was sizing up Friederike quite uninhibitedly. "Did she get that from you?"

"I think so."

Michael raised his eyebrows warningly. But they certainly got further when they played with their cards up. "Of course, we're talking about my work. And after the Oxford conference..."

"Together we're writing a book about it. That gave me the idea of how we could combine work and dance. Here." Michael pointed to the dance hall.

Tanja looked suspiciously from Friederike to him. "You're about to plan an attack!"

"If that's what you want to call it," Friederike said. Marga suddenly stood motionless, a bottle of water in her hand. Friederike suppressed her comment about it; that would not be wise now, "A project for courtly dances of the Baroque. If some people are willing to participate, the board will certainly support it."

Werner shook his head. "Too expensive. No one could afford the costumes. And where are they supposed to come from anyway?"

"There's a huge medieval festival in Querfurt. I've been there before." Axel got eager. "They sell costumes there, too."

"Middle Ages!" Ines snorted. "Well, that's really old!"

"But don't most dances come from that era?" Axel looked around questioningly. "Shouldn't we know that more precisely when we dance? Where all this comes from?"

Christina shook her head. "I don't need to know how to build a car to drive it."

"But somebody has to know!" Axel gave Christina a provocative look. "Otherwise you wouldn't have a car to drive in the first place."

Christina shrugged.

Michael raised a brow again. Christina could actually rain on their parade. Not here in the circle; the zeal in the faces of the others spoke for itself. But if she worked Werner at home, he would tell the board that the club had no money for it. Did they have to maneuver here just as much as in the faculty?

"Actually, I'm interested too," Tanja said. "I'll buy your book." Her smile widened. "I'm sure you'll need subscriptions to get it published." They didn't really need them, but that wasn't important now. Selling more books was always good. "We'll make a flyer and advertise it here at the club. And wherever we meet other dancers in the near future."

"Thank you." Friederike's gaze went to Michael. Now it was his turn again.

"We've come up with a special highlight for the book. One of my friends could produce a video CD to go with it – if he had something to record."

"Film, you mean," Axel said.

Michael nodded. "Since we're not able to travel back in time. In music, this is constantly done by producing original musical examples with the original instruments."

Tanja's face began to glow. "I'm sure we can borrow the costumes for the gig. We'll ask at the opera. Or at Babelsberg." Excited, she twisted her hair. "Or at the *Friedrichstadtpalast*?" She turned to Marga. "Do we have anyone at the club who has contacts?"

Marga shook her head. "Something like that is not in the membership records. You'd have to ask."

Tanja put her left hand in her hip. "But you know everybody! I'm sure there's nothing you don't know about."

Werner's mien became grim. Tanja must have put her foot in her mouth. "We're jerking Marga around way too much already; don't make her work for this, too."

Marga put her hand on his arm. "Thank you, Werner. But let it go. I'm happy to help if I can. You know that." She smiled at Tanja. "First, see if you can get this Baroque story done at all. Then we'll see where we can get the costumes."

"Also borrowing the costumes costs something." Werner looked even darker than before; for sure he now felt rejected. Though he just meant well. "For how many dancers anyway? For Chris' troupe or more?"

Tanja looked at Friederike questioningly; Michael answered for her: "Just see, how many dancers you can get excited about it."

"How many couples? Divisible by four?"

He looked at her for a moment, puzzled, then understood. "It's not all quadrilles."

"Very well. There's definitely Axel." Tanja pushed her index finger into her brother's chest. With the help of her fingers, she began to go through the substitute dancers they had in square dancing at the moment.

"So you can almost open a third square," Marga exclaimed from the background of the bar.

"No one cares about that now," Tanja chided her.

Friederike was surprised by the hostile vibes that suddenly emanated from Tanja.

Marga didn't seem to notice; she just shrugged. "It was just a thought that suddenly went through my head."

"But it'll cost too." Werner sighed audibly. "It would be good if our groups continued to grow. More members bring more dough to the club. But it also costs more for outfits."

Tanja looked at him with her head tilted at an angle. "It's good to know that the club wants to contribute to the cost of our costumes in the future."

Werner widened his eyes. That was probably not what he'd meant - that witty Tanja... But they shouldn't embarrass him too much now; otherwise he'd see his wife's objection as a lifeline and vote against the idea.

"My research budget is sufficient to cover the cost of recording the CD." It wasn't a lie phrased that way. She was certainly allowed to say that to end the discussion about the costs. "But the time the dancers put in..." Friederike regretfully raised her shoulders. "Tanja, we don't have a budget for this."

"But it doesn't matter," Michael said. "If the additional effort is too great for you, we'll make students from our faculty do it."

Friederike was almost having a stroke. Students – teaching them the dances took far too long if they had no previous experience. They needed the square dancers. And also those from the Latin formation would learn fast enough, because they had experience in dancing synchronously.

Michael's gaze went from one to the other. "I'm sure Madeline's ready to train the boys and girls." Madeline, however, was the one person who had the least time of all so shortly before her *Abitur*.

Eventually he looked at Friederike again with an almost insidious grin. He had something in mind! Of course he had. She should really trust him.

Tanja supported her chin on Axel's shoulder. "Of course, we both could dance together. Like here in the dance circle. To my own brother, Micky will surely lend me for a short time." She gave Michael a look; that look was quite something. "Micky's my partner in square dancing."

She turned to Friederike. "You and Madeline, you're gonna clear this with George. I'll take care of the costume rental and you, Michael, will organize the movie production." She smirked. "Maybe we could use a director, too. We're gonna saddle Chris with this job; he's already bossing us around anyway."

10

The following Monday, Tanja had secured the ballroom in Berlin's Castle Schönhausen for the shooting and the German Opera had approved to lend thirty costumes. The reference to Friederike's scientific reputation impressed the director of the opera so much that he was even prepared to ask the State Ballet for dancers if the Lietzensee Dance Club did not have enough. As a result, half of the Latin formation was ready to participate as well.

And then suddenly everything was teetering on a knife-edge. Hans-Dieter Friedemann, the coach of the formation, fueled Werner's fear that their successful participation in the regional league's promotion tournament would be in question: The formation would not have enough time for the "real" practice. Werner frightened the board with the prophecy of impending bankruptcy. As a result, George also objected to the project.

The day after this turbulent board meeting, Micky hacked into the club's computer and got the phone numbers and email addresses of the formation dancers who had volunteered. Tanja called one after the other and told everyone not to worry about Friederike's publication: They would just add the dancers of the State Ballet to the square dancers. That, however, was something no one wanted. Even George thought this would be a disgrace to the club.

At the following board meeting he fumed about the interference of the coach. Wasn't he, George, the one who did all work for the club? So how could Hans-Dieter get in the way with his petty misgivings? The Latin formation was first-class; they knew their choreography in their sleep. Did he doubt they would ascend and win the Northern Championship? He should rather see to it that Rita Färber got a partner who could replace Frederik, who had died in an accident...

Given George's outburst, Werner suddenly remembered that the budget had never been calculated in such a way that the club depended on the tournament successes of its dancers.

George came home very pleased with himself. "The club supports your work, Rieke. I have removed all obstacles." He related how the board meeting had gone.

"I was sure I could count on you." Friederike let him take her in his arms. She knew very well what maneuvers Tanja had arranged to get the movie going. "You all put a lot of effort into standing up to Hans-Dieter."

George burst out laughing; then he kissed her on the lips. "No one had to assert themselves against Hans-Dieter. I reminded him that the board makes the decisions." He nibbled on her lower lip until she opened her mouth and let him in. George had become more affectionate since she danced again. It certainly wasn't a coincidence. But maybe it was just a result of his jealousy of Michael?

She put her arms around his neck and stroked his nape. "If I didn't have you..." Oh, how she hated that maneuvering.

✳✳✳

On Saturday at nine o'clock in the morning they stood in the large hall of the Lietzensee Dance Club: the entire square dance group including all the substitute dancers, five couples of the Latin formation, Tanja's brother Axel and two other gentlemen from the dance circle for the substitute dancers who had no partner. And the Heinemanns – for whatever reason they had come.

Chris, of course, had agreed to serve as the master of ceremonies, which a part of the dances required. He would never have thought of resisting Madeline's request.

Before they danced, Friederike and Michael provided a summary of their book. They titled it "The First Globalization of Art". Friederike's part dealt with the development of regional folk and peasant dances into dances of the nobility, which then were danced in the same way at all courts of Europe. Michael on the other hand wrote about musicians like Andrea Falconieri, who traveled from court to court and everywhere picked up local melodies for their compositions and adapted them into dance music.

Friederike had just finished her presentation when Tanja jumped up.

"I have an idea!" She looked around the room for applause.

"Alas!" Axel put his hands in front of his face. "What threatens us now?"

Micky laughed. "Tanja's ideas are the best!" The look he had for her was full of admiration. But Tanja didn't seem to notice.

She pointed to the wall on which Friederike had just projected her pictures. "We need more costumes!"

Axel moaned theatrically.

"Of course! I only got courtly costumes at the opera. But that won't work. We also need peasant costumes. Or bourgeois – whatever."

"She's right," Micky said. "If we want to illustrate development, we have to dance in peasant costumes, too."

"But it costs twice as much money!" Werner Heinemann

crossed his arms in front of his chest: "I said right from the start that the club could not finance such extravagances."

"But the costumes cost us almost nothing," Madeline protested with flashing eyes. "Can't that get inside your head that Tanja did magic? And that Grandma's faculty has a budget for it anyway?" Which, of course, they should not make use of to not give Carlsen any ideas. But that didn't belong here now.

"But that only applies to Friederike's film. And what about the open house day performance? We want to use it to improve our cash position, not ruin it."

"We'll cross that bridge when we're getting there," Chris said. "You have not yet made a decision in the board, let alone a date under consideration."

And they had come to dance that day, not to argue. Friederike turned off the laptop and turned on the CD for the first dance: A branle from the 16th century. The conversations ceased; the first ones began to sway to the beat of the music.

"What?" Norbert Kaminski of the square dancers suddenly shouted. "But that's from the *Bots!*"

Michael laughed. "It's an old Breton drinking song. The *Bots* have used the melody in their '*What do we want to drink?*'"

"A processional dance?" Axel asked in a shy voice. The boy meant it seriously; he really wanted to know where the dances came from.

"At first. During the development to courtly dance jumps and other ornaments were added. It's one of the first dances for which the steps were written down." Michael held out his arm to Friederike.

She restarted the piece and then they first danced the simple step of the *branle double*: left foot to the left, right foot closing... and the same to the right. Then, in conclusion, they decorated the sequence of steps with a jump on the left foot while stretching the right one forward. Afterwards instead, they jumped a "capriole" with both feet: the right leg in front and the left leg behind.

"This looks nice. Very – elegant." Madeline smirked and turned around to the square dancers in general and Chris in particular. She pulled him onto the dance floor and before the piece of music was over, she had learned the step sequences with him.

Madeline grinned like a Cheshire cat. "It's very simple." She pushed her elbow into Chris' side. "Easier than square dancing." Which of course wasn't true.

She danced another capriole. "In what language are the commands actually given?"

"There are none at this dance. It's really simple. You only need a master of ceremonies for very long, very varied dances like the quadrille." Friederike smiled at Chris. "One of the forerunners of square dancing."

"Commands also exist in some folk dances," said Michael. "For example, the Scottish-Irish céilì, which are still danced today."

"That would be a nice project, too," said Christina Heinemann. "I love old Irish folk music."

Well, that was a surprise. Christina suddenly got excited? Friederike had thought she had only come for her husband's sake. And Werner's concern would be controlling the project.

Friederike played the piece again. Meanwhile Michael went in front of the men and she in front of the ladies and they practiced the first steps with them. It was exactly as Friederike had hoped: Most dancers not only mastered the steps very quickly, but were also able to dance them in sync with the other couples.

Michael eventually stood next to her at the stereo and watched with his head tilted. The dancers were practicing jumping the fifth step of the galliard with crossed legs and appearing elegant at the same time. "This is gonna be great, Rieke. I'm imagining it right now in the castle."

By lunchtime they had agreed on the sequences of steps for branle and galliard, which they wanted to learn for filming. Michael ordered pizza for everyone, Madeline took over the bar and they spent a fantastic hour together, Friederike and Michael telling about their research.

Michael leaned against the wall next to Friederike. "Your club really is a great troupe."

"Our club." She laughed at him. "Better than hiring a group of students."

He contorted his face like he'd bit a lemon.

"That's what you suggested."

"But Rieke, you actually don't know anything about tactics. That really surprises me now."

"Speaking of tactics. Have you been able to figure out when Carlsen is planning his release?"

"He doesn't have a secretary I could bewitch. After the stunt Karin put down for him with the *Call for Papers*, they're all extremely cautious."

"Are you trying to tell me the grapevine has stopped working?"

Michael just shrugged and followed the dancers into the big hall. Next on their agenda was the quadrille.

In a dance break later in the afternoon, they showed excerpts from historical movies and drew the dancers' attention to how the heavy courtly costumes influenced the movements.

"The head will be the hardest part." Tanja was bursting with laughter and began to parade with a stiff neck, as if wearing one of these imposing, uncomfortable wigs of the 17th century.

"Where do you get *mouches* these days?" asked Rita Färber.

"Theater supplies," Kirsten Schneider, another dancer in the Latin formation, suspected. "Later we could use these for ourselves. They just have to be big enough to be seen across a dance floor."

"Do you want to distract from your missteps?" asked Gregor Buchenhain, her partner.

Laughter rang through the room.

"I thought you were dancing," came George's voice from the hallway. Then he stood in the door frame and let his gaze wander. "I was bored at home, like a grass widower. So I thought I'd go see how you were doing."

Did that sound like control? Anyway – there was no reason not to be happy about his appearance. "Oh, George, that's wonderful! You'll be thrilled." Friederike greeted him with a kiss on the cheek.

When they resumed their practice, George took a chair from the office and sat next to the stereo.

But George's presence was distracting. The fact that he constantly frowned did not contribute to relaxation either. The others seemed to feel similar to Friederike, because suddenly everyone was moving much stiffer than before. They blundered at the simplest steps.

They had wanted to rehearse till six. But at five, Michael turned off the music. "That's it for today. I think we've reached a point where any more would lead to confusion." Surely none of the dancers had heard such a thing before:: They were used to rehearsing until a step was in place. Or they would tilt out of their dance shoes from exhaustion.

The wrinkles on George's forehead deepened considerably and he hissed disapprovingly. As if it were any of his business!

"We've done a lot today. You guys are really great." Friederike thanked practically everyone individually with her glances. "We will certainly need less time than we expected."

Of course, George had to say something too. Just so no

one forgot who he was. He shocked everyone. "It doesn't look difficult. But of course, folk dances had to be like this so everyone could dance them immediately." It was downright insulting how he belittled their work. "Even I dare to dance that right away."

Friederike was perplexed; she couldn't think of anything.

But Michael suddenly had mischief in his eyes. "We shouldn't miss that." He winked at Chris and went to the stereo. "Part of the quadrille once again, together with George."

Friederike didn't even want to know what a face George was making now; instead she studied the row of ladies. "Micky, let George take your place." Tanja was just the right partner for him.

Tanja pushed Micky a step to the side and stretched out her hand to George. With a quiet groan, he peeled himself out of his coat, buttoned up his jacket and took Micky's place. At least he accepted the challenge.

"Well then," Michael whispered in Friederike's ear. At Chris' nod he pressed the start button.

Chris picked up the microphone. He began with the second dance of the quadrille. *"L'été": "En avant deux – en arrière – chassé. à droite – chassé à gauche..."*

This sequence of steps allowed George to watch two other couples first and then it was little more than simply stepping forward and back to the position and a *chassé* with alternating steps. The art consisted in appearing prim by head and arm postures also as a man.

George had become heavy in recent years and had never paid too much attention to this aspect of dance expression. They were lucky to be working with a Latin formation. The expressive bodywork, they were accustomed to, allowed the dancers to quickly acquire Baroque mannerism. However, the square dancers had also held up well. Madeline had probably aroused their ambition to show that square dancing was as professional as the rest of the Lietzensee Dance Club program.

For the next dance, George had no direct role model. Michael counted the steps while Chris announced *"La Poule"* in his odd sounding French. *"Traversé – retraversé – balancé – demi-promenade -- en avant deux – dos-à-dos..."* But George proved that he had watched attentively before. He even managed to change partners without delay.

Tanja honored him with a look of pride. "George, it's a shame you stopped dancing. You'd still be good."

Michael audibly sucked in the air.

Tanja shouldn't be giving George any ideas! Anything but that subject now. The project had been brought to life with so much effort; a single breath of wind could sweep it away.

Friederike was awfully tired of maneuvering. Maneuvering, continuously maneuvering. At the faculty. At the club. She didn't have to have that at home, too.

After the quadrille Madeline left the formation and put her arm around Chris' hip. "It was a bad idea to appoint you our master of ceremonies. We haven't been able to dance together in ages."

He laughed and kissed her on the tip of her nose. "Was that your secret ulterior motive when you suggested the Baroque dances?"

Madeline giggled. "I'll think of something new." She sat on the floor and changed her shoes. "Grand... Rieke, we also need matching shoes. Have you thought of that?" She held up her dancing shoe and looked at it from the side.

Kirsten took Madeline's shoe away and held it in front of her partner's nose. "Can you even stand on that? Or walk? Dance?"

Those two were right. At that time the shoes for men and women had been the same: high heels for the nobility. They couldn't just arrive with them on the day they started shooting. "We should actually train the gentlemen so they're used to moving around in them."

Werner grimaced. "More money." But now that they had started, they had to do it right.

Tanja clung herself at Werner's arm. "Didn't you recently promise that the club would subsidize the costumes? Why not start with that?" She fluttered her eyelashes innocently.

"Because you'll only need those shoes once."

"Twice," Madeline shouted. "Once for – George's wife," and she emphasized that unmistakably, "once for the next open house day."

"The one the board hasn't planned yet." Werner looked even grimmer than before.

Lydia Aydemir swung her red cowboy boot. "Can we go home now, or will we dance some more? My husband would love to see me for once."

"We're going to the pub," Hinnerk shouted; he was meanwhile standing at the bar with a beer in hand. "Call Sakir; he can even come on foot."

Pub was a good idea; but what did she do with George during that time? Friederike exchanged a look with Michael, so that he understood he should definitely go with them.

George caught her gaze too. And misunderstood it. "You want to go to the pub, Rieke? Don't you need the time for your manuscript?"

She could have strangled him. "I didn't mean to; what makes you say that?"

He stared downright hostilely at Michael. Right. That was exactly why she didn't intend to go.

Michael left the dance hall and came back immediately, his coat over his arm. "Same pub as Fridays?" He waved to Friederike. "On Monday, you'll have my comments on the manuscript."

Madeline let Chris help her on her feet and then wrapped

her arms around his neck. "You dare go into the lion's den without me? I'm leaving with Grandma. I've got to do some cramming."

Chris put his face in her hair and said something that made her face glow. The sight of these two was always beautiful. Friederike could not imagine that one day it would end between them, as George constantly prophesied. If she and George had had more in common than dancing like these two had... or more than a child... then their happiness would not have been so terribly clouded after the accident.

The dancers put on their street shoes and then one couple after the other made their way to the pub. George and Werner disappeared into the office. They closed the door behind them, but soon after it was unmistakable that they were arguing.

Friederike drank her wine and slipped from the bar stool with an angry growl. How did they dare to keep them waiting here until they had fought their battle.

"Grandma, let's go to the pub. Certainly somebody's gonna get us home."

"Of course. Michael would do that for sure." And continue to fuel George's jealousy. – Without knocking, she opened the office door. "George, give me the car key. Then you can finish up arguing without haste and I can do my job."

George had probably already been furious due to the confrontation with Werner. Now he looked like he was about to go for her throat. That man and his moods!

Friederike lowered her outstretched hand. "Or we could go to the pub after all." She turned around and waved to Madeline, who then put on her coat.

They had only arrived on the first landing when the door was opened and George called for her. Madeline grinned at her before Friederike turned around.

"We're done." Werner's face appeared behind George's shoulder. Bright red; he was apparently upset too.

Once again she felt like at university. Here, too, it was a matter of asserting one's own mind. And what made sense counted for little. No wonder the club had to fight for its existence.

11

At home, George put the car key on the chest of drawers and took Friederike in his arms before she had even taken off her coat. "Rieke, that was brilliant!" He took her into the courtly dance posture he had just learned; their hands raised high. He led her with prim steps into the living room, where he let her go with a leg bow.

"Just like old times." She took off her coat, put it over the back of the couch and sat.

"I'm imagining the costumes for it. It'll be great fun." He went to the closet and took out the cognac bottle. "You too?"

She nodded. After the exhausting day, she could take something to relieve the tension.

He handed her a half-filled glass and sat next to her. "It's easy enough even for me old bones to keep up."

"What do you mean by that?" George wanted to dance galliards and quadrilles? With her? That didn't work; it would guarantee a disaster. They hadn't danced with each other in sixteen years. Except the one rumba at Carnival. Hectically she looked for an idea how to dampen his zeal. Once George started, he wouldn't rest until he had the whole project in his hands. But it was not a project of the club. Did he forget that in his exuberance?

"Didn't you just say I'm still learning as fast as I used to?" George suddenly had mischief in his face. "I shall surprise the young people."

"You need a partner." She frowned. "I don't have time for this."

"But today you danced."

She nodded. "Of course. We wanted to offer more than a few old pictures and clips from 'Angelique'. Michael and I will take turns in the future; none of us has time for all the rehearsals. I have four weeks left to get the manuscript to the publisher."

Now he looked seriously shocked. "But until then... Then Hans-Dieter is right: Your dancing is colliding with the rehearsals of the formation. You'll have to practice for hours each and every day." Angry, he clenched his fists. At that moment she considered him capable of changing sides again.

Before he could ask her to cancel the project, she began to laugh. "George, you should have listened better some other time when I was preparing publications. It takes at least until spring before the manuscript is ready for printing. We have months left to practice." Oh dear! As soon as she had spoken the sentence, she realized that she had now shot herself in her foot.

"Then why don't you have time to dance anyway?"

She sighed. "With the submission the manuscript is not done. Who knows what the publisher wants to get changed?"

George frowned. "But what do you have to rehearse? Since you teach the dances, you can already do them!" In view of George's zeal, she became more and more queasy. He was actually obsessed with it. Did he now seriously want to start dancing again or was it just this unusual project that attracted him? She needed time to think how to handle it.

"You're right about that, of course." She snuggled up to him and kissed him. "Let's just try how to do this." Better she ended the subject now. Otherwise he would get so stuck in the idea that he would rather risk the whole project than refrain from dancing himself.

"It'll work out." George's hand went under her hair and he stroked her nape "And if I need more time than the others to dance in sync, we'll save it for the open house day."

"So you've decided this now?"

He squirmed somewhat uneasily. "On the board, we haven't even talked about it. But who would object?"

"Werner?"

Georges groped for the zipper in her back and pulled it down a bit. His fingers were circling on her right shoulder blade. "Did he say anything?"

"Well..."

"I know. Werner always sees only the expenses; not what income could arise from them." He shoved the dress off her shoulder. "But we don't have to discuss that right now."

"Truly not." It was not really her business what the club later did with what the square dancers and the formation were learning now.

She'd have to call Michael and tell him George wanted to dance with her. Then what? Wouldn't he think that was the first step of getting rid him? The Moor has done his duty... But she had promised Michael not to let him down if George should come up with the idea of dancing himself again. She'd keep her word.

12

When Friederike arrived at the faculty on Monday morning, Michael's notes on her manuscript were on her desk. She briefly leafed through the folder: not much and nothing essential. Hardly more than a day's work.

She started the computer and in the meantime sifted through the snail mail. Another *Call for Papers*. A conference next autumn in Toulouse, organized by the *Musée du Vieux-Toulouse*. It would certainly be nice to participate. But conference language French?

She called Michael in his office. "Do you speak French?"

"*Bonjour, madame.*" He laughed. "*Où est la gare?* I find my way around. Do you want to go on holiday in France with me?"

"You won't believe it: yes. Something like that. Next fall there will be a small, and probably fine, conference in Toulouse."

"Autumn is good. We can escape the students for a few days."

"So you know French well enough to engage in discussions?"

Michael grumbled something, then sighed. "I used to be really good at French. With a little practice... And you?"

"Then we'll practice together."

This time Michael's sigh was clearly theatrical. "What has happened to your family's Huguenot heritage?"

"Good thought! We'll have Madeline correct the paper. She's our language genius."

Shortly afterwards Michael came into her office and got a copy of the *Call for Papers*. "Why didn't Tom send this to me? Does he have a new scheming secretary?"

"Ask him!"

"I'd rather not. If he's wearing out his secretaries because of us, he'll kick us out."

He can't, she almost said. But only she had a civil service job. Michael's contract may have been unlimited, but that didn't mean anything anymore. "Perhaps he believes that the Huguenot legacy is mine and not George's. How should he know you speak better French than I do?"

"Well, doesn't he read my research?"

She laughed. "Weren't your sources for Oxford all in Occitan?"

He placed a hand on his heart and put on a face as if she had wounded him deeply. "You don't read my research either. Otherwise, you wouldn't have missed the French sources."

"I actually read your works, but not your literature lists."

"Back to the subject: You mean we should attend?"

"Is there anything against it?"

"Good. We'll go. Toulouse in September is fine." He leafed through the documents, read individual passages and frowned more and more. "If I can think of a theme for it."

"But Michael!" Why did this man have so little confidence in his abilities? He'd have made a career long ago if he'd been braver.

He grinned. "You're probably right again. I'll think up something."

Think up something, that was the cue. "George is pestering me about our movie." And she still didn't know how to brush him off without endangering the whole project.

Michael questioningly raised an eyebrow.

"He wants to dance with us." She held her breath.

"And what did you say?" Michael's face was blank, but the

tension in his voice betrayed him anyway: He wondered how long it would take for George also to want to dance the ballroom dances with her.

"That we have to see first how things are going." She shrugged to give the impression of casualness. "George has never been able to conform. It will torture him to dance in sync with others."

"Then he could be at the dances that don't require it." Did he really not mind? She was looking in his face for a sign what he thought.

Michael was suddenly smirking. "Now you want to be able to read minds. Don't you trust me?"

"And you - do you trust me? I'll remain your partner in the dance circle, no matter what George thinks up someday." Was that the solution to the dilemma that loomed in front of her? Dance circle with Michael and Baroque with George? She didn't dare ask what he thought of the idea. Michael would have to figure it out for himself: Only then would she be sure that he thought it a good solution.

"I know you meant what you said. But can you keep it up?"

He thought she was that compliant? She was shocked – and hurt. But wasn't he right? Hadn't she wished for sixteen years to dance again with George? Michael deserved honesty.

"Gorge is now far too old to seriously think of competition dancing."

"But he wants to dance again. It's obvious."

"He would never lower himself to a dance circle." She started tidying up her desk to find time to think.

Michael chewed on his lower lip. Obviously, he was thinking, too. "Because the level in the dance circle would be a step backwards compared to what you used to dance? This Baroque story, on the other hand, is new territory..."

Friederike laughed; relieved that Michael's thoughts seemed to go in the same direction as hers. "Absolutely. However,

George has so far raged against any attempt that went beyond the World Dance Program."

"It's a miracle he tolerates square dancing."

"Because otherwise he would have lost some of these dancers completely to the club. Tanja's parents, for example, would never agree to pay the dues for two dance clubs."

"Wouldn't she have stayed because of her brother?"

She laughed. "He doesn't need her that much now. And she herself is rightly of the opinion that she can dance enough to keep up everywhere."

Michael looked at her questioningly.

"Like Madeline, she has no further ambition."

"I see!" He smiled. "The future female doctors and architects will only learn for their professional appearance."

She nodded. Should she come back to George? Better not; Michael shouldn't think she wanted to force the issue. Since she herself had put George off to wait. "Back to Toulouse."

He went through the documents again. So fast, he certainly couldn't read anything. "Let's do it! This is a great opportunity to show our movie, too." He chewed his lip again. "We can even consider the convention when we shoot the movie. In selecting the dances we record. They learn so fast, it may as well be one more dance."

Good thought! "This invitation comes at just the right time."

"All we have to do now is get it all right."

"For that," she waved her copy, "we even had almost a year to learn." What if they could make more of it? An invitation to the Lietzensee Dance Club? Live instead of a movie?

13

In the evening, the program director of her publishing house called Friederike at home. "Mrs. Lagrange, I just read your letter." He was literally breathless. "This movie is a great idea! That takes the publication to a whole new level..." Chewing sounds came through the phone. With that call, he could have truly waited until after his dinner. "However – I imagine that to be difficult. How are we going to finance it?"

She was at a loss what he meant and waited for an explanation. But he seemed just as eager to get an answer from her. "A blank CD costs... how much? Don't you think you could ask two more euros for the book than originally planned if you had the CD with it?"

"With this print run, that doesn't cover the additional expenses."

"What additional expenses do you have? The plastic bag for inserting the CD?" She rolled her eyes; what a cheapjack. "An acquaintance works in a music publishing house. I can ask him how much it costs."

"But Mrs. Lagrange! What do you take me for?" She'd rather not tell him. "I'm talking about the cost of producing the movie. The salaries."

"Oh, if that's what it is! We've been through everything; don't worry. My husband's on the board of a dance club. And the dancers are pleased with the change." She waited a moment to see if he had anything to say to it. He didn't. "Otherwise, I would have enclosed an estimate."

His answer was incomprehensible; probably he was just thinking aloud. If he couldn't decide... Now they had the conference in Toulouse in prospect. This made the project definitely worthwhile; even if the Lietzensee Dance Club did not take it up permanently as an additional offer. And for two euros the students would buy the CD anyway.

"Mrs. Lagrange, I'll discuss this with Mr. Weyring in the morning. I'm sure I can give you the green light afterwards." As if they depended on it. Or waited for it. Bureaucrats!

After they had arranged a phone call for the following afternoon, Friederike fetched a glass and the open bottle of Burgundy from the fridge. She decided on an ancient Truffaut movie and wrapped herself in a blanket on the living room couch.

An hour later, George came home from his board meeting. After filling his glass, he sat next to her, took her feet into his lap and started massaging them. "How was your day, Rieke?"

"Interesting. Next year there's a conference in Toulouse..." She told him about the idea of winning the museum for a public event. "...and Weyring shall give his blessing to our CD tomorrow."

"Shall give. What does that mean?"

"He won't know of his luck until tomorrow. The program director is a little afraid, but he wants to make it palatable to him."

"When do we have to have learned all this?"

"It depends on how long it takes them to produce the CDs. Christmas, I guess."

"Christmas?" George sat up straight. "Oh, that's good. The board has decided to organize a New Year's Eve ball with a program." He smiled mischievously. "Instead of an ordinary open house day."

"With program?" And Werner had blessed that? But they needed a stage then. She couldn't imagine it in the club rooms. If the big hall were full of guests, there wouldn't be much room for dancing. And if there was enough room for dancing, there would be little room for paying guests. Then the ball wouldn't bring in very much.

"We'll rent the Zenner at Treptower Park. It's located just fine. Imagine how the fireworks will reflect in the Spree." George became more and more enthusiastic as he spread out the details of the program to her. Surely he had also wiped Werner's concerns off the table in this way. "Of course, your Baroque dances will be the highlight before midnight." He rubbed the bridge of his nose thoughtfully. "Speaking of midnight! We could organize it as a masked ball, don't you think?"

As a masked ball! Did he forget the Carnival ball? Her stomach knotted in the memory of Madeline's raging.

"Oh!" Georges raised his eyebrows; then he started to laugh. Obviously, he remembered, too. "It was Marga's dance cards, not the masks." Well, might be true.

"We'd need Venetian masks for the Baroque costumes." But certainly they were also available in some pool.

George knocked an imaginary beat on her left foot. "Then we'll do this as a masked ball." He beamed like a little boy. She hadn't seen him in such high spirits in a long time. Maybe it really made a difference whether he could dance himself or not. Which would become her dilemma, should it occur to him that he didn't want to limit himself to her project. Her project? Thoughtfully, she ran her fingers through her hair.

"Hey, this place is reserved for my fingers." George took her hand and kissed the palm. "What are you hatching about having to pull your hair like that?"

"It sounds like the dance club could do a lot with the Baroque dances."

"Yeah, sure. If we'd even perform somewhere else..." He looked at her questioningly.

Would it be better if she didn't say anything else now, or was it wiser to use his current enthusiasm? "I'm just thinking."

"You do that all the time." He bent over and gave her a kiss on the tip of her nose. "And what is it this time?"

"There are some among the dancers who are as enthusiastic as you are. Couldn't you open up a new group? Or does it draw too much energy from what they're actually dancing?"

"You mean an additional offer?" His face didn't tell her what he was thinking. She now had to let him think it through undisturbed until he had an opinion about it; then they could discuss it. Otherwise, he'd feel pressured. "Werner won't know how to finance this."

Why did everyone talk today about how much it all cost? "But people pay for individual courses or training hours in addition to the membership fee."

"Yes, of course; but we must keep these fees as low as possible. And the basic contribution is not designed to have a lot of people making use of everything." She could understand that. Otherwise the club could not at the same time allow for moderate fees as well as propose a varied offer.

"But when the rooms are free, an additional group could use them and thus make a small contribution to the rent."

George had no objection to that.

If the club opened up to new ideas it would be good for the budget. They had to win young people if the club wanted to survive. With the ballroom dances alone, it didn't get far anymore.

14

The answer to Toulouse still had time to be sent, but Friederike announced to Tom that they wanted to participate. Did Carlsen actually speak French?

He could, Tom said. And he pointed out that the faculty council could not simply favor them again. "The faculty can't afford to lose Carlsen to another university."

Did this mean that Carlsen had received a call to another university and was now conducting negotiations to stay? Then they had to tell the faculty council about their dance movie to be unrivaled.

Swearing inwardly, Friederike went back to her office and spent the next three hours researching which universities had publicized for which professorships. If she found something suitable, Michael had to apply and then also conduct negotiations to stay. They could spare him even less than Carlsen – at least Tom saw it the same way she did.

She hated these machinations; but it seemed she hadn't bothered with them for far too long. And not played along for even more. Michael would declare her crazy if she went to him with this. He couldn't scheme well either, but it had to be done. In the end she had three vacancy notices that had not yet expired. Michael would certainly never take one of these jobs. But they were good for putting pressure on the faculty council.

In the afternoon she went to his office to discuss the revision of her manuscripts. She took the notices with her.

To her surprise, he asked her to negotiate an earlier publication date with the publisher.

She studied his work plan for a while. "That doesn't work, Michael," she finally said. "We can't finish the CD that fast. People have to learn everything first."

"They're good; you saw that on Saturday. Let's turn the half-day appointments into whole days on the weekends. Then we can do this."

"Why are you in such a hurry all of a sudden?"

Michael sighed. "The grapevine... Carlsen allegedly put his manuscript into the mail this morning. Someone saw a big package addressed to Herkomm Publishing."

"To Herkomm?" She stared at Michael in disbelief. "This is a publishing house for the general public!"

"I know. But what difference does it make?" He was smirking. "Except he thinks his material isn't sound enough for scientific publication."

"But Michael!" How could he be serious? "It means he'll try to do both. The more difficult work just postponed."

"Sure. He is probably working first on his guest lecture for Freiburg. I saw the expense claim."

"He gets his travel expenses reimbursed from here to apply for a chair in Freiburg?" That was cheeky!

"He's not applying to Freiburg."

"How do you know?"

"The faculty head called me. They're holding a symposium in December and they wanted to invite me." Why was he only telling her this now? "I told him I don't have time. Our joint project comes first." And then, as if he could read her mind, "That's why I didn't tell you."

That was an explanation, of course. But not a good reason. "Why don't you let us decide together if you can reconcile both? It's one more chance for you."

"Chance of what? I have no intention of leaving Berlin. At

best Potsdam would be an option. Berlin is still an exciting city; I wouldn't want to miss any of it."

Then maybe she shouldn't come up with the idea of fake applications. If he raved so vehemently about Berlin, others knew that too. They wouldn't believe him for applying anywhere else.

"Whatever," he went on. "Now it's too late. Carlsen is going instead."

"Couldn't you have imagined that?" Just what was the matter with Michael? Didn't he ever, ever think about how to advance his career? Suddenly she was angry. "But you do realize that this will also improve his standing here with us?"

He shrugged. "I don't measure myself against other people. For me, what counts are the students and that I enjoy my work." He smiled mischievously. "Just like our dance project. It's really great that I'm bringing everything together that's important to me." Sneaky flatterer!

Friederike still shook her head exasperated, but her anger subsided enough for her mind to gain the upper hand. "If only Carlsen couldn't harm our plans. Just imagine if he was exhausting the travel budget of the faculty!"

"The museum in Toulouse pays the expenses of those who they invite."

"For one of us, yes. And the other one?"

"Now let's write this paper and then we'll have to wait and see if they even want to invite us." Which was guaranteed after their success in Oxford. After all, that's why she'd gotten the *Call for Papers*. From whom, anyway? She should look at the list of participants again; obviously she had overlooked at least one of the French. She would see to it that Carlsen did not again run rings around them like in Oxford.

Michael looked at the clock. "I have to go to the seminar. And then I'll start thinking about that." He waved the papers from Toulouse.

Now she hadn't said a word about the fake applications. Should she do it? She was still undecided. Maybe she'd rather concentrate on her work than on scheming. She wasn't very good at that anyway.

15

Three days later Friederike sat in Michael's office with a bottle of champagne. Weyring had done far more than take up the proposal with the dance CD: Next summer they would present their translated book and their work in the USA.

Suddenly the door was thrown open and Carlsen stormed in. His hair stood on end, as if he had been tearing at it for hours, and his face was red.

He looked from Michael to Friederike and back again. Then his gaze got caught on the champagne bottle. He put his fists to his hips. "Then I guessed right."

Friederike smiled at him. "You guessed we were gonna sit here and have a glass of champagne?" She raised an eyebrow. "And I thought I carefully covered the bottle when I came in this morning."

Carlsen blew up his cheeks. Really and truly, he looked like a balloon. "You! For fifteen years, you've been anxious to ruin my career. But I won't put up with that any longer. I'll see to it that you two don't get another leg to the ground."

"What happened, Professor Carlsen?" Carlsen did not react to the suggestive tone in which Michael used the title.

But he got even redder in the face. "You stole my publication!" He got louder and louder. "First you oust me at Oxford, now Kurinski Publishing."

"Oh? You were going to publish with Kurinski? Mr. Weyring didn't say a word that he was in contact with you." So he had seriously thought about rewriting the material for the

Oxford conference and publishing it a second time. And imagined Weyring wouldn't know. Carlsen seemed far from thinking that this could be the reason why the publisher did not want his book.

As dismissive as Michael scrutinized him, he probably had similar thoughts. But why did Carlen think they were responsible?

"I won't forget that!" Carlsen was actually able to inflate himself even more. Probably getting high on his anger.

Michael got up. "Mr. Carlsen, you should leave. Your behavior is unacceptable."

Michael's calm seemed to upset him even more. He kneaded his fists and struggled for air.

Over the years, she had seen quite a few of Carlsen's acts; but this exceeded everything. And just because of a problem with some publisher? No way. There was more to it than that.

Michael opened the door and pointed out with an unmistakable movement.

Carlsen tried to stab Friederike with his gaze before he turned to the door.

Two students came laughing down the hall. At Michael's door, they slowed their pace. One of them greeted Carlsen politely; but the raised eyebrows clearly said she was puzzled. She had certainly never seen her professor so deranged.

The redness in Carlsen's face deepened. "Yes, well..." he murmured. Then he hastily left the office.

Michael closed the door and leaned against it. "What was that?"

Friederike pointed to her manuscript. "Can we finish this today?"

With a quiet laugh Michael came back to the desk. "It's not much anymore." He leafed through the manuscript until he came to the penultimate chapter, "Just this is left..." He suggested some additions because several people in the dance club had wished to learn the Breton gavotte as well. Michael thought, then they should also take shots of it and explain.

"It boils down to a full dance class if you go on like this."

"It's fun to teach others how to dance." Suddenly he froze, surprise in his eyes. "What is it? You look like I just found the Philosopher's Stone."

Maybe he actually did. She grabbed his arm. "Would you do that on an honorary basis?"

"Like this now?" He grinned. "Why not?"

"Not like now. Not so intense, but longer." She smiled at his surprised look. "Paying the coaches makes it so difficult for the club to warm up for new groups or courses. Marga... rent... what do I know... It's all expenses that are incurred anyway. But coach hours, they all count extra."

"Even if it means Marga's working more hours?"

"Marga doesn't look at her watch. She stays in the office a lot longer than she should anyway. I think she needs this."

"We should neither approve nor support that." The laughter lines around his eyes deepened. "Rieke, where's your union spirit?"

She giggled. "You mean my class consciousness? In this case, I'm unfortunately on the side of the exploiters."

"Back to the manuscript." Oh! He had nothing to say to that.

16

Two months later they began shooting in the ballroom of Castle Schönhausen.

Square dancer Carola Maaßen was responsible for the hairstyles. She came with a teacher and three students from her hairdresser class at the vocational school and they devoted themselves with zeal to their task. With hair pieces and lots of accessories they prepared the dancers' hair for the courtly part of the film. Since the wigs used in many historical films had in fact only been in fashion for a relatively short time, they had decided against it for the female dancers. But the male dancers had to wear them, because none of them had hair long enough to tie it in the neck.

Tanja had decided to use Rococo costumes. The *poches* attached above the hips were more comfortable than the spherical Baroque hoop skirts. And the pastel-coloured, low-cut dresses were much more beautiful than the puritanical garments of the High Baroque.

Friederike got a pale green dress with a richly embroidered bodice, a deep rectangular neckline and elbow-length sleeves, which continued in airy needle lace - the *engageantes* - over the forearms.

Michael's friend Peter Kornfeld came in the late morning, when most of the dancers were finished with their hair. He brought a camerawoman, his script supervisor and a make-up artist with him. His string quartet consisted of music high school students who had bent backwards for the honor of appearing in the film. For each dance they had learned several pieces and while Peter was installing the technical equipment, they chose together with Chris what they would play.

George beamed like a little boy when he realized after a short time that everyone was working with the highest professionalism. After he had put on his costume and been made up, he practically didn't leave Peter's side anymore. But he interfered very little and almost all of his suggestions made sense.

They danced the *Contredanse Française* twice to the quartet's music, then it got serious. Peter switched on the spotlights and the camerawoman turned on her camera; the script supervisor held his clapperboard in front of the lens. "One - the first."

Chris put his feet closer together than he usually did and at that didn't seem like a square dance caller anymore. With this small change of posture he actually managed to give himself an air of courtly manners.

"Le rond." The eight dancers in each square gave each other their hands and danced first to the left, then to the right in a circle... *"Le moulinet des dames."* The female dancers gave each other the right hands in the middle of their squares and turned clockwise; then with the left hand going in the opposite direction... *"L'allemande."* The couples crossed their hands in their backs and hand in hand finished their turn with a rigaudan step... *"En avant et en arrière."* They made a gavotte step forward and a gavotte step back...

Michael stood a bit away from Chris next to Peter and had the shooting stopped if mistakes were made. Friederike were dancing with George in the same square as Madeline, who had Axel as a partner. George often had his gaze more with the other dancers than with Friederike; but he did well. Only twice did he take the first step after Axel had already started to move.

Michael didn't seem to have seen it and kept them dancing. So Friederike thought. But then Peter made repeat the dance George had messed up. Likewise later another one, who was not good enough for Michael either.

In the end they had danced five of the nine "stanzas" of the *Contredanse Française* to Michael's and Peter's satisfaction.

"How many weekends did you have planned?" George asked.

Now Friederike didn't want to tell him that - this shooting lasted much longer than she had expected. "I'm sure we'll make do with four weekends."

George wrinkled his forehead.

"But yes," she said with as much conviction in her voice as she managed. "Once we'll dance in peasant costumes, we'll need a lot less time for dresses and hairstyles."

"Even if we only have one hour more a day, it makes a difference," Peter said. "You'll get routine, too." He took down his spotlights. "Where are we going to eat, Michael?"

For lunch, George and Friederike joined Michael and the filmmakers at "Richter's im Tschaikowski-Eck", a restaurant in the old Berlin style that was only five minutes away from the castle. George was in his element for good when Peter began to question him about his past career as a tournament dancer.

"Dance school — is it still profitable these days?" Peter finally asked.

"We're a club, not a dance school. Even though you can learn to dance with us." He explained to Peter at lengths the difference between schools and clubs; of course he trivialized a little the competition that existed between them.

Peter had followed his long explanations with undiminished interest. When George was finished, he leaned back, a contented expression on his face. "I could pitch this to RTL.

You know the network produces these dance shows. By now a background report should be of interest to viewers."

George reached for Friederike's hand. "I guess you'll have to deal with the publisher who'll publish my wife's book."

But Peter waved it off. "I don't want that movie, not this one. I'm thinking of a movie about the dance scene in Berlin. With your club, if you like. – Of course, whether something will come of it depends on whether I get the assignment from RTL."

George squeezed Friederike's hand even more; he seemed to control his excitement only with effort. Free advertising on a renowned network! That would be so much more than a simple open house day. Or the intended New Year's Eve ball. "How soon do you need our decision?"

Peter raised his shoulders. "If it could be soon?"

"We can decide at the next board meeting on Tuesday. How can I reach you?"

"Through Michael, of course." Peter smiled. "I understand that he's a member of your club, right?" But then he reached into his wallet and pushed a business card over the table to George; he really meant it.

George studied it before he put it in his pocket.

Michael got up. "Let's continue!"

When they went back to the castle, George linked arms with Friederike and held her back. "I'm glad you talked me into this adventure."

"Werner won't know what hit him."

"His eyes are gonna pop out." George made a grim face. "And Hans-Dieter's, too." Then he stopped and kissed her tenderly.

END

If you liked this novel, please recommend it. Recommendations and reviews help others to find books worth reading.

About the author

Annemarie Nikolaus began literary writing at the beginning of 2001. After publishing several short stories, her first novel was published in 2005. She now publishes her work independently.

She was born in Hessia/Germany and lived in Northern Italy for 20 years. In 2010, she moved to Auvergne, France with her daughter.

She studied psychology, journalism, politics and history and worked as a psychotherapist, political advisor, journalist, editor and translator, among others.

You can find Annemarie on Facebook: www.facebook.com/
AnnemarieNikolaus.Autorin
and Twitter: http://twitter.com/AnneNikolaus

If you want to know, when more of her books are available in English, then sign up to her newsletter.
http://eepurl.com/bHQtvf

***

Publications in English:

Magical Stories. Short stories for children. Paperback edition ISBN 9781479157037.

Radiant Hope. Illustrated science fiction story. Paperback edition ISBN 9781484977163.

Past Crimes. Historical crime short stories. Paperback edition ISBN 9781507136744

Silenced. Short thriller. Paperback edition ISBN 9781507176238

Deceased. Short Stories. Paperback edition ISBN 9781507190371.

Aquitaine: The End of a War. *"By The Wayside..."* series. Non-fiction. Paperback edition ISBN 9781507141861

Other dance novels:

The Granddaughter

Madeline Lagrange loses her heart to square dancing – and to the group's caller.

Chris Rinehart, the caller of the "Lietzensee Dance Club", falls for Madeline. Yet out of a sense of responsibility he denies her his feelings.

While Madeline tries to seduce Chris with all the intransigence of her seventeen years, her grandfather wants to expel him from the club.

Falling for a movie star.

Tanja Walters' secret love is her square dance partner Micky Hasloff. But when the dancers are hired for a Western, she flirts with the star of the movie, Manolo Rioja.

Out of jealousy Micky sabotages the shooting. Only a meeting with Rioja and his wife convinces him that not the star stands in his way, but his own fear. Now does Micky dare to reveal his love to Tanja?

Quick, quick, slow – Lietzensee Dance Club
– Dance Novels –

The idea for these "Dance Novels" was developed by the author group "Schreibwerk". The stories are set in Germany in a fictitious Berlin dance club during the first decade of this century.

Each book in the series can be read as a stand-alone.

At present, only Annemarie Nikolaus is getting her novels translated. In addition to English, currently available are translations into Italian, Spanish and Greek.

You can find out more (in German) in their blog .https://schreibwerk-news.blogspot.com/p/blog-page_28.html

Annemarie's novels:

Die Enkelin. Also in English, Italian, Spanish and Greek.
Zurück aufs Parkett. Also in English and Italian.
Flirt mit einem Star. Also in Italian

Other authors:

Tine Sprandel: **Der Treppensturz** and **Nele**.
Marion Pletzer: **Tanz bei offenen Türen**
Evelyn Sperber-Hummel: **Liebe tanzt Rumba**